Award-winning and international bestselling author Ashley Fontainne enjoys stories that immerse the reader deep into the human psyche and the monsters lurking within each of us. She writes in numerous genres including mystery, suspense, horror, sci-fi and sometimes poetry. Two of her novels, *The Lie* and *Ruined Wings*, are currently in production for feature films. Find out more by visiting her website at www.ashleyfontainne.com

Ashley lives in Arkansas with her husband and is the proud mother of one son and three daughters.

@AshleyFontainne
/ashley.fontainne

MARRIAGE MADE ME DO IT

ASHLEY FONTAINNE

KILLER READS
A division of HarperCollins*Publishers*
www.harpercollins.co.uk

KillerReads
an imprint of HarperCollins*Publishers* Ltd
1 London Bridge Street
London SE1 9GF

www.harpercollins.co.uk

This paperback edition 2017

First published in Great Britain in ebook format by HarperCollins*Publishers* 2017

A catalogue record for this book
is available from the British Library

ISBN: 978-0-00-826690-5

For Rebecca Roberts – voice talent extraordinaire,
relentless cheerleader and amazing friend

CHAPTER 1

This Is The Life I Wanted, Right?

Ignoring the droning voice of the old man talking up front, I let my thoughts wander. As usual, they went back to my youth. Growing up in the Seventies and Eighties, I was blissfully ignorant of how screwed-up my life would turn out when I reached the A-word: Adulthood.

I'm the oldest sibling of three girls born into a middle-class family. We grew up living in the suburbs, safely hidden from the dangers of "the big city." God, life back then had been a breeze. We walked to school, without fear of stranger danger, on sidewalks wide enough for three people to stand side by side, with shade provided by sprawling oak trees. We played with our friends—outside, mind you—until the streetlight in our cul-de-sac buzzed, ready to come on. We didn't have electric gadgets to tether us inside, weakening our bodies and turning our minds to mush. Nope! We survived skinned knees and bike wrecks, eager to go out and do the same thing again the next day after school. We'd run to the house and land on the porch before the streetlight sparked to life and eat a home cooked meal at—of all places—the dinner table.

We weren't rich, like my best friend Elizabeth Gelmini's family—they had a swimming pool and a tennis court, for Godsakes, and both her parents drove BMWs—but we weren't poor, either. Since I was the oldest, I got the new clothes, and my younger sisters, Rebecca and Rachel, were forced to wear my hand-me-downs. Boy, do I miss the days when Rebecca whined and complained while stomping around in her Pepto-Bismol-colored room throwing hissy fits as only a pre-pubescent girl can.

"I don't want Roxy's clothes! Look, Mom! There's a stain on these jeans. And this shirt is so out of style! No one wears puffed sleeves anymore! I'll look like a fool and all my friends will laugh at me. Why can't I get a new pair of Calvin's or Jordache's? Tennis shoes without holes in them, or even the latest design of a shirt?"

"Rebecca Denise, that's enough. Money doesn't grow on trees, you know. Your father works very hard to provide a good life for you girls so I can stay home and raise you. Stop being so unappreciative. I didn't give up a chance for a career in nursing just to listen to an ungrateful child yell at me."

"Mom! I can't wear her shirts. Roxy's big boobs stretched them out! I'll have to stuff my bra!"

The memory made me smile, which I quickly concealed with my hand. This was not the place or appropriate time to be happy.

I glanced over at Rebecca. Though her features had matured and changed, her attitude certainly remained the same. Rebecca was the quintessential middle child. Textbook case. Hell, her picture was probably underneath the caption "Middle Child Syndrome" in every psychology book on the planet. If it wasn't, they were missing out on the perfect poster child.

Cosmos, forgive me, but I've hated her ever since the day my parents brought her whiny ass home from the hospital.

Mom and Dad lived by *The Suburbia Handbook*. Roger and Claire Rayburn built their lives around the ancient, mental code of ethics. Mom and Dad almost nailed Rule Number Two, chapter and verse.

All married couples must procreate and raise, at a minimum, 3.2 children, preferably staggered in ages by three years.

They missed the target goal by having offspring of the same sex. They needed at least one with a set of balls to pass with flying colors. Unfortunately, the estrogen pool was deeper and stronger—or perhaps Daddy's sperm refused to bring forth another knuckle-dragger into the world. Who knows? But, they made up for missing the bar by acing Rule Number One:

High school sweethearts must marry; the wife is to stay at home and raise the children while the husband brings home the bacon.

Nailed it.

Like my mother, I aced Rule Number One—the track star married the football jock. Boom! Item number one checked off the list. I didn't count the demerit (we *had* to get married our second year of college). Getting married at 20 wasn't because of overwhelming, all-consuming, mind-altering love. Nope. I tied the knot with Carl A. Davenport because I neglected to read the instructions that came along with the prescription—taking antibiotics *might* disrupt the effectiveness of birth control pills.

Fuck. I got knocked up at 20 because of a freaking sinus infection.

Demerit!

No, wait, I wouldn't count that one. It was the manufacturer's fault—they should have written that part in big, GIANT print, rather than using letters so small one could only read with a microscope.

Carl continued his studies and obtained a master's degree in education and was now a tenured professor at the local college. Me? I gave up the dream of going back to school, following the guidelines of the invisible handbook passed on to me by my mother. I was a "stay-at-home Mom" (better known as *Drunk Wino*). I tried to follow the rules, but sometimes missed the mark. No one could ever label me an overachiever!

Rule Number Two altered a bit during the Nineties—inflation

and such—and the required number of children went from 3.2 to 2.5 (unless you were a devout Catholic and preferred to birth an entire baseball team). I failed Rule Number Two and only popped out one child—a daughter— who decided I was the Wicked Witch of the West, minus a broom, when she hit puberty. Hormones turned my sweet child into a raging alien life force. Thank goodness Carol planned to attend college in a few weeks or our home would be a demilitarized zone.

God, I really miss Carol being little. My daughter is a replicated copy of me. Carol had dark, thick black hair; alabaster skin; long legs and full lips, and thankfully, a rack smaller than mine. Carol had been an inquisitive child, full of life, a sweet laugh, and boundless energy. A tiny shadow stuck to my side, mimicking everything I did. That lasted until Carol hit the age of 5 then poof! My clone rebelled, running in the opposite direction of my life. I sensed the disturbance in the force, so instead of attempting to indoctrinate Carol's mind with the rules, I simply hoped she'd follow them later in life, after watching me from a distance.

Wrong.

Carol Claire Davenport put as much distance as possible between my world and the one in which she desired to live. Headstrong, and determined to succeed in life without a man's help, paying her own way through life, and—gasp!—hiring help to perform such trivial tasks as cleaning or cooking, Carol bucked tradition every chance she had, including phases of punk haircuts, head-to-toe black clothing and makeup (for a while, it felt like Morticia Addams lived in our house) and refusing to clean her room. My little straight-A student and lovely mixture of introvert and extrovert wanted nothing to do with my "old school ways" as she liked to refer to how I lived my life. Carol idolized her aunt Rachel's free-spirited approach to life, and jumped at every chance to spend time with Rach when she was in town.

Had I wanted another brat—er—offspring—I was shit out of luck. My ovaries opted to shrivel up and die not long after Carol was born. Maybe my body had the ability to see into the future and knew I couldn't handle raising another bundle of flesh I'd give up my life for only to have him or her turn on me the second puberty hit. Yeah, that was it. Thank God for omniscient reproductive organs! There is a clause in the *Handbook* noting bodily failure in Rule Number Two, which kept me from accruing a demerit.

Score!

I took after my mother's side of the genetic pool. Jet-black hair, long legs, and boobs the size of ripe watermelons. Everyone else adored my full chest, but not me. Carrying all the weight around—every freaking day—was painful. Running track was dangerous. I had to wear three sports bras just to corral the heavy flesh so I didn't bust an eye socket. By the time I was 25, back problems surfaced, along with my preferred method of numbing the pain: Drinking wine. That little lesson landed on my doorstep, courtesy of Mom and Grandma. I watched them down wine like it was fresh mountain water all my life. Of course, they preceded the wine with handfuls of pills—Valium for Grandma and Xanax for Mom—a tradition I didn't follow.

Other women flocked to their nearest plastic surgeon to get implants to look like me, which I found rather amusing. Why, oh why in the world did they do it? Personally, I think it should be required pre-surgical treatment to strap two, 10 lb weights on their chests for at least a full month. Get the entire "heavy breast experience" prior to undergoing the knife. Just one month of being forced to sleep on their backs, trying to find a bra that fits, enduring catcalls, and never having a man look you in the eye while speaking—ever again—would deter most. Give them a real taste of what to expect, before having some cocaine-addicted surgeon slice into their milk dispensers so they could then afford the newest Mercedes to drive around town.

Rule Number Eight: *One must always drive a vehicle that is better than the ones owned by friends and neighbors.*

(This is not a guideline it's a hard-core edict! See Rule Number Nine about houses, too).

Then again, maybe the wretched experience with strap-on boobs wouldn't matter. The media had ingrained its warped perception of beauty since the dawn of the big screen and TV. Boys were indoctrinated with ridiculous, impossible body types as their ideals, and young girls learned to be ashamed they weren't "perfect" every single time they looked in a magazine, watched a movie, or plopped in front of the boob tube. Ah! Lightbulb alert! Boob tube—an appropriate name! And who paid for this mind-altering phenomenon? Not the men. They reaped the benefits of unhappy girls who went under the knife.

Pathetic.

I sought out, and found, a surgeon to reduce my oversized chest, much to the dismay of my husband, Carl (yet another young boy whose views of beauty were warped by media-generated garbage). For the first time since puberty dumped too many hormones into my breasts, I could walk around without a bra on and it didn't look like two baby hippos were fighting under my shirt. Hallelujah! After going from cup size *Holy Shit Those Are Huge* down to *Gee, I'm No Longer Carrying Fucking Watermelons On My Chest—Just Nice Oranges*, I continued my relationship with wine. Why the hell not? Several glasses of Moscato each night kept me from acting out my sick, knife-wielding fantasies on those who'd pissed me off one way or another.

Though I wore the persona of a normal, well-adjusted person for others to see, inside my mind had always been a different story. Even when young, I learned to fake the smile and serene demeanor when faced with adversity, only unleashing my real emotions inside. Rather than slit the throat of my fourth grade teacher for dressing me down in front of the entire class over what she perceived as a "less than stellar" book report, I remained quiet. After school that day, I went home and took out my anger on one of Rebecca's favorite dolls.

Adhering to the strict set of proper and correct rules for living, I refrained from punching in the throat—or worse—rude cashiers, snarky friends, impatient waitresses or any shorttempered individuals within my hearing range. Instead, I satisfied my dark, demented thoughts of retribution by simply envisioning my reactions.

Ol' middle sis Rebecca didn't have the same worries, for her body had been dipped in the pool of mishmash genes from my father's side of the family. Shorter legs, smaller breasts, dingy brown hair, and an attitude the size of Texas. Oh, and Dad's horrible eyesight. When she found out she needed to start wearing glasses—the kind as thick as Coke bottles—Rebecca Denise Rayburn flew into the biggest, ugliest, snot-filled tantrum of all time.

It was hysterical. I laughed so hard while she bawled and squalled like a newborn kitten, Dad grounded me for a week. Those seven days of banishment to my room had been worth the few minutes of hilarity at Rebecca's expense.

If I had to pinpoint the moment our sisterly relationship curdled like sour milk, it would be the day she came home with enormous frames swallowing her small face. I teased her nonstop for hours until she sobbed. And no, an additional week of grounding didn't faze me in the least.

Things were never right between us again. We'd fought before, but after the incident of the poor eyesight, it was full-on war. Roxy versus Rebecca was probably foretold by some ancient sage—detailing the apocalyptic event between two strong-willed, mean-as-fuck women.

Not that I gave a rat's ass. Rebecca was a bitch. A raving, I'm-off-my-meds, lunatic bitch. When the song "Lunatic Fringe," by Red Rider hit the airwaves in 1981, I changed the title and words to "Lunatic Bitch," in honor of my insane sister. Rebecca didn't stick to the rulebook completely. Yes, she married her high school sweetheart right after college, but she went to work immediately after graduating with a degree in accounting. Bucking tradition, Rebecca paid the bills while her hubster finished med school.

Demerit.

Rebecca earned another bad mark for not giving birth. Mom gave her—and Rachel—grief for years to give her grandchildren. Apparently, my single contribution wasn't enough. Before Mom's mind traveled to a new dimension, she'd whine and bitch about how *all* her friends had *several* grandchildren to spoil.

Demerit. Demerit.

Rachel, on the other hand, was the best sibling ever created from the union of an egg and sperm. Ever. She was kindhearted, full of smiles, never a complainer, which was sort of odd since she was the baby. Rachel was a free spirit, flitting from one moment to the next, distracted easily by a light wind, never one to hold a grudge. Rachel wasn't as tall as me, yet had a similar build. She'd been born with an ample chest, thick, mahogany hair, and generous curves.

Out of the three of us Rayburn girls, Rachel was the animal lover, though Rebecca attempted to keep up, yet always failed (i.e., Rebecca neglected to remember animals need to eat or they die). Every baby bird on the ground, abandoned cat, scrawny stray dog, half-dead hamster—they gravitated to Rachel's sweet soul. Like some cosmic connection, a weird instinct guided them to head directly into her path. And sure enough, Rachel Danielle Rayburn scooped them up and brought them home, much to the dismay of our parents.

I didn't have any lovey-dovey, sisterly, protective feelings toward Rebecca (again, Lunatic Bitch), but boy, I sure did with Rachel. Instead of getting caught up in the Eighties' drug scene (like Rebecca and I both dabbled with—Lunatic Bitch snorted so much she had to stop and have surgery for a deviated septum—ha!)

Rachel was the exception to the hedonistic lifestyle embraced by most.

Looking back on it now, it was kind of like Rachel was an old soul meant to be in her teenage years during the Sixties. Rachel would have been the perfect flower child, right at home in Haight-Ashbury, wearing flowy dresses, her dark mahogany hair dotted with flowers as it billowed around her sexy body. Well, a flower child minus the drug part. To my knowledge, Rachel never got high or drunk. Life, and all it had to offer, was enough stimulation for my baby sister.

God, I miss her so much. It isn't right. Carol and Rachel were my two reasons for living. Rachel should be here, sitting on the stiff, uncomfortable pew, mourning the loss of one of her screwed-up sisters, not the other way around. Rachel's life ended with eerie finality before the age of 35, damn near close to how Dad always said it would: Animals would be her downfall.

Rachel's ill-fated stint working undercover for some whiny, ASPCA-type sacks of shit, ended her life. While trying to save a dog from being put down, Rachel suffered a wicked bite. Instead of going to the doctor immediately, she waited until infection set in—and rabies. For two weeks, doctors fought to save her life, yet failed. The only Rayburn daughter to toss *The Suburbia Handbook* to the wayside and live in—gasp!—the big city, was dead. I hate myself for thinking it, but I'm sort of glad Dad passed on and Mom is lost inside her mind, wandering the locked hallways of Dementia Hotel.

No parent should have to bury their child. It was wrong—a crime against the natural progression of the way the world was supposed to work.

Rebecca pinched my arm, drawing me back to the funeral service. With a nod of her head, she directed my attention to the center aisle. If I wasn't half-bombed on wine, I would have stood and said something. Opened my smart mouth and given the worthless piece of shit shambling toward the casket an earful of my internal thoughts. Maybe kicked him in the crotch with my high heel, laughing, while he fell to the floor clutching his busted ball sack.

A funeral to remember!

Instead, I simply glared at—oh, shit, what's his name? I just drew a total blank, which makes no sense. Carl always said he admired my elephant-like memory, though I believe that was a Freudian slip—Carl meant he admired my elephant-sized mammary glands.

Aha! The little panty-waste's name is Benny Rogers, Rachel's boyfriend. Gaunt and pale, he looked like a walking corpse. All he needed were some bloodstains and rotting skin to complete the look. Wisps of mousy brown hair stood up in all directions, his thin chest covered in a disheveled white dress shirt, tan khakis sagging around a non-existent ass. Some artsy-fartsy emo kid who spent his time and money on animals rather than buying things like deodorant or clothes that fit. The boy was a real winner. The kind of date you brought home to meet your parents just to cause a massive heart attack or stroke.

Memories of conversations with Rachel popped into my head. She'd gushed over the phone about her new boyfriend, how he'd helped her see the light about the plight of animals that were tortured and lived short lives full of nothing but pain just so we could eat them. Benny convinced her to become not just a vegetarian, but a freaking vegan.

A vegan! If Dad wasn't already dead, the knowledge his youngest child refused to eat meat would have sent him to the grave. Nobody loved throwing animal flesh on a grill more than Roger Rayburn.

Nobody.

Rule Number Four: One must cook meat outside over hot coals (or propane if you're lazy) and invite all friends and neighbors to partake of said charred flesh. This act must be done at least three times each month during pleasant weather.

Dad missed the fine print which noted health concerns and advised to remain healthy in all other areas so as not to clog the arteries.

Oops.

Lunatic Bitch agreed with me for the first time since out of diapers, so we tag-teamed Rachel. Nothing we said changed her mind. In less than six months, she'd dropped so much weight, had the same gaunt, pale skin as Benny-Boo (her nickname for the sack of shit, not mine) Rebecca and I feared she was ill from lack of consuming animal protein.

"He's got a lot of nerve showing his ugly face," Rebecca whispered. "He needs to leave. It's his fault Rachel's dead! He's the one who convinced her to go undercover and risk her life—over freaking animals! Plus, he convinced her to quit eating any type of meat. It made her body weak and that's why she didn't respond to treatment. He doesn't deserve to be here. Wait, that's not true. He does deserve to be here—inside that casket, not Rachel! Thank God, Mom's not here to see him."

"Mom's not here because she doesn't even know she's our mother or her youngest child is dead. She's a drooling, forgetful mess. You're a heartless bitch, L.B. Heartless."

Rebecca bristled. "I am not! And stop calling me that! Little Bit was cute when I was, like, 2, but not now. You're the oldest and have Dad's attitude, so you should do something! Make him leave."

Despite the fact my beloved baby sister's funeral was underway, I smiled. The little lie I'd told years ago when questioned by Dad about the meaning behind the nickname "L.B." still stuck.

Wow, I am a sick, twisted wench who loves her petty torments.

Carl nudged my arm. "Shhh. The pastor isn't finished with the service yet."

Glancing over at my husband of close to twenty years, a spark of anger burned inside my chest. Carl Davenport sat next to me, all serious and sad, like a proud pimple on the ass of humanity.

Though still quite handsome for his age, Carl's thick, brown hair I used to love running my fingers through during heated sex was gone. What little hair he had left was all gray, including the newest addition to his sharp facial features: Long, white, obnoxious hair in and around his nose and ears. The little tendrils stood erect and strong, forcing your eyes to stare at them with disgusted awe.

Seeing Carl's new, unnecessary hair, made me think about my own. Mine opted to sprout in areas hidden by clothing—thank God! Several thick, black pubic hair follicles became lost, choosing to take up residence around my nipples and right underneath my belly button. No amount of waxing, plucking, or shaving helped. My next plan of action was a blowtorch.

The strong, sexy muscles from his youth weren't quite a fleeting memory yet, though dangerously close (similar to my once tight ass). Carl sported his own ripening watermelon right above the beltline. When we did get naked under the sheets, the sweaty monstrosity full of itchy hair rubbing against my body made me sick to my stomach. Thank goodness, Carl discovered Internet porn and spent most of his free time behind a closed, locked door in his study. Naked, pixilated sluts on a screen kept me from fulfilling, for the most part, Rule Number Ten:

Housewives must service their husband's needs when the man's urges overtake him, no matter how tired, sick, in pain, or stressed the wife feels.

Carl's admonishment to remain silent worked just the opposite: It gave me the needed push to act a fool. So, of course, I did.

"That boy isn't welcome here. Look, he's up there saying his goodbyes to Rachel while the preacher is talking, and you're giving me shit for whispering? Talk about disrespectful! Dad's not here to toss him out the door but I am!"

"Roxy—wait!" Carl whispered.

Ignoring my wimpy husband, I stood and stomped with purpose down the aisle. Several mourners gasped, and the preacher's words dried up. Grabbing a handful of Benny's collar, I pulled him backward, bringing his ear inches from my lips. "Leave, now, or I swear I'll make you wish your daddy had shot blanks. I'm not even kidding. Better yet, I'll make sure you shoot blanks from now on after I slice your balls off."

Ol' Benny-Boo shook like he was in the midst of his own personal earthquake.

Sensing his fear, I let go and he turned and disappeared through a side door. Satisfied with myself, feeling a rush of power at releasing some of my pent-up anger, I walked back to my seat.

Carol and Carl looked mortified, their faces pale and mouths agape. Rebecca beamed with pride. We didn't see eye to eye on pretty much anything, yet on this particular rule, we did.

Rule Number Eleven: One must defend their family, no matter what. This rule trumps everything else. (In my mind, I added a footnote: *Even if the defense comes in the form of bodily harm to another.*)

Once back in my seat, the preacher decided the service was over, and music filled the sanctuary. Tears welled up in my eyes. I should have acted on Rule Number Eight's footnote sooner. Instead of trying to talk some sense into Rachel, I should have concentrated my efforts on forcing her to eat red meat and removing Benny's eco-friendly ass from her life.

Permanently.

While those in attendance to the final adios of Rachel Danielle Rayburn stood and ambled outside, I remained stuck to the pew. Something sinister bubbled up inside my chest, worse than a wicked case of heartburn after eating fried foods.

Replaying Rachel's entire life inside my head, watching memories zoom by of the life we once led and the one I hoped we'd continue living, made the mental safety valve break. Fury burned through me for failing to take care of her better. I didn't keep the promise made to my mother years ago to watch over and care for my younger sibling. Mom seemed to recognize Rebecca could take care of herself and that Rachel was the neediest one of her three girls.

And for some reason, Mom thought I was the nurturing one. Pft! Joke's on her!

Looking down at the remembrance card with Rachel's sweet, happy face staring back at me—a picture I picked out from ones taken in our backyard last year—I swallowed hard, forcing my pain and sorrow deep inside. I'd failed my sister but there was no way I'd make the same mistake with my child. Despite all of the hormone-induced struggles during the past two years, Carol Claire Davenport was the reason I was put on this planet. With Rachel gone, all of my attention would be on Carol.

God help any fool who dared harm a hair on my precious child's head.

I whispered a silent vow, promising to not make the same mistake again. Rachel's death made me question the *Handbook* I'd used as a mental guide my entire life. While "Amazing Grace" filled the small room, I decided to alter the rules to suit my world. I was sick and beyond tired of it being the other way around.

I swear, Rachel, the next person who tries to disrupt my family—they won't be granted a reprieve. I'll do whatever necessary to keep the rest of us out of harm's way. I promise.

CHAPTER 2

Don't Bite The Hand That Feeds You

Our slice of Heaven on Earth, a large McMansion with four bedrooms and three baths (Rule Number Nine—check—thanks to Carl's wealthy family!) built on the backside of the suburbs I grew up in, was crammed full of people. Fancy cars filled the tree-lined streets. A smorgasbord of all sorts of metal chariots driven by grieving guests, ones insistent on paying their respects by trudging through my house, stuffing their faces with food, spilling wine on the expensive hardwood floors. Cleaning up after the invasion would be fun. Not.

Rule Number Fifteen: A woman's job as housewife is to maintain a pleasant, always spotless home for her family.

Joy.

The display of food made me hate Rule Number Twenty:

When someone dies, you must put on your best clothes, your saddest face, and pay your respects. This act must be accompanied, of course, by a homemade dish to feed the mourning relatives of the recently departed.

Freshly prepared food had been replaced by stopping at any given superstore and buying a tray of assorted meats, cheeses, and vegetables. My kitchen table and counter looked like the deli aisle.

"You outdid yourself with the service. It was beautiful. Of course, I had no doubts it would be, since you plan everything out to the minutest detail, even when overcome with grief. You've always been such a rock."

The voice of my best friend Elizabeth (and neighbor, three doors down) made me smile. Elizabeth and I had maintained our friendship since second grade, and she was the only person in the world I truly trusted.

Rule Number Seventeen: Have a best friend to lean on, gossip with, shop, drink, cry to.

Check!

"Thanks, Liz. I still can't believe she's gone. It hasn't really sunk in yet, you know?"

Liz nodded while picking up a tray of full wine glasses. She nudged me aside. "Here, let me. You look tired, and it's not your job to cater to these fools. They are supposed to be helping you get through this, not looking for a free meal and drinks. Go and have a smoke out back. I can tell you need one. Oh, and listen—Sasha just told me she canceled book club this week. We'll pick up next Friday, okay? Give those dumb hags who always complain they haven't finished the book time to do so. Maybe we can actually discuss the book rather than listen to them gossip."

Shoulders sagging with relief, I smiled. "You're a gem. Is she here? I haven't seen her."

Liz frowned. "Honey, you seriously need to get some rest. Better yet, let me get Roger to give you some pills that are guaranteed to knock you out for a week. Your mind is on the fritz from all the grief."

"What do you mean?"

"She's still out front talking to Mr. Shock, just like you were less than three minutes ago."

Annoyed by yet another silly game of Let's Confuse Roxy that people had been playing on me during the last few months, I said: "Today's not the day to mess with me, Liz."

A wounded look creased her brow. "I'm not joking, Roxy. You were *just* talking to her. Lord, did you get any sleep at all last night?"

"Pft. Sleep? I haven't had time to do much of anything except plan a funeral. Not even sure I put deodorant on today, so I'm not surprised a superficial conversation with Sasha and Mr. Shock slipped my mind. It doesn't really matter. I'm not in the mood to listen to her today, so please tell her I'm grateful. I've been looking forward to the discussion. It was our first ever erotic romance, so things might get really interesting! I'll be right back. If I don't inhale some nicotine, I'll snap."

Elizabeth's perfectly waxed eyebrow lifted in curiosity. When surprised or amused, Elizabeth Gelmini Rosenbaum was downright gorgeous. "I thought you already snapped once today? From my perspective in the back, it looked like Rachel's boyfriend got an earful of foul words. I didn't think it was possible for him to be any paler. Boy was I wrong."

"Men don't take being threatened with castration very well," I answered, chuckling. "He's damn lucky the alcohol in my system saved his little nutsack from getting whacked off."

"Roxy!" Liz gasped. "Shh! Save that sort of talk for when we're alone!"

Heat raced to my cheeks. Normally, I only let my demented thoughts escape my lips within hearing range of my bestie. "What can I say? It's been a really difficult two weeks. Better to only say my sick thoughts than actually commit the act, right?"

"True."

Rebecca strolled—no, she wobbled—up beside us. During the last hour, I'd counted six glasses of wine disappear down her throat, compared to my measly two. She was a drunken mess, which wasn't a first. An intimate relationship with alcohol was another thing she'd inherited from our parents. Of course, I did too, so I really couldn't count that as a demerit against her or I'd have had to add it to my bag as well.

Good thing she lived only a block away, or she'd take out anything and everything in her path driving the enormous SUV Stephen bought her last year. The Escalade sported every single option, and even had a personalized license plate with L.B.'s name on it. Er, well, her *real* name, not my preferred name for her. (Score one for Stephen and Rebecca Wilson—they passed Rule Number Eight with flying colors!)

The fancy silk dress she'd purchased from Nordstrom for just this solemn occasion, the perfectly applied makeup and stellar hairdo (thanks to some very expensive trips to the salon to attach extensions probably made from horse hair!) didn't hide the fact ol' L.B. was bombed.

Pointing a well-manicured finger behind her, Rebecca muttered, "Uh, Roxy? You might need to pay more attention to Carl. He's ogling the Shock's daughter again. You know, Cherrywood Estate's resident Kardashian wannabee? Guess in the midst of his sorrow, he's forgotten Coco's underage. Maybe you should go remind him before he gets into trouble? If Mr. Shock catches a glimpse of the eye-fuck Carl's giving Coco, he'll beat your worthless hubby within an inch of his life."

Liz gasped, gave me a sheepish smile and then turned tail and headed to the living room to pass out more booze. I contemplated asking her to come back and give me the tray so I could storm over and dump it on Carl's crotch to cool the blood heading south.

What little love I had left (and it was little—close to the size of a pea) for Carl from all of our years together vanished. Rage made my fingers tremble. How could he? At Rachel's wake?

It would take a lot for me to best Carl physically, so I turned the brunt of my anger toward Coco. Taking her down would be a piece of cake and oh-so enjoyable. Visions of wrapping my fingers around the girl's slender neck, squeezing until her fake face turned three shades of purple, filled my mind. Oh, better yet! Grab a handful of the expensive, blonde extensions recently purchased by her mother, Elaine Shock (because her daughter was going to be "a famous model" after getting a nose job, silicone-infused lips, fake, *human* hair, and bonus! saline-filled breasts) and drown the little whore in the pool.

No, that wouldn't work. Those knockers were buoyant. Drowning the skank was out of the question.

Coco. Who the fuck names their kid such a ridiculous name? Wait! I know the answer! A former beauty queen who married some real estate mogul, gained about 50 lbs, and spent the remainder of her life living vicariously through her daughter's body, and had an obsession with Chanel.

Yep! Nailed it!

My cravings for nicotine disappeared. It was overshadowed by raw fury. Rebecca was right—Carl stood at the edge of the den while Coco leaned against the doorframe, her gazongas dangerously close to escaping the thin material covering them. And where was my husband's gaze? Laser-beam focused on the boobs.

Not in my house, in front of our friends and neighbors.

No. Fucking. Way.

It was one thing for Carl to self-abuse himself in front of a computer screen, drool and sperm shooting out of him like a 14-year-old boy, while staring at pixelated images. I'd learned to live with Carl's porn addiction, but this? Practically popping a boner during Rachel's wake? If left alone any longer, he'd start humping Coco's leg.

"Excuse me, L.B., I'll be right back."

Rebecca downed the remainder of her drink, smearing the last traces of red lipstick, and laughed. "Let me know if you need help burying the body. Those breasts and her enormous ass added on at least twenty pounds. After all, what are sisters for if not to help hide a crime? You already look like a serial killer in that cheap dress. Seriously, Roxy, you could have at least bought a designer label for Rachel's funeral. It's disrespectful to look so damn frumpy."

Pulling my gaze away from my pathetic spouse, I glared at Rebecca. An apocalyptic comeback brewed inside my head. Lowering my voice, I whispered: "If I had any doubts before about you being the reigning Queen of Shallow People, you just wiped them away. Allow me to let you in on a little secret. L.B. means Lunatic Bitch. Always has."

Expecting an angry response, Rebecca surprised me by laughing so hard she farted. "Oh, I can't wait to tell Stephen! That's his pet nickname for me in the sack! How funny is that?"

"Fucking hilarious," I replied with a smirk.

Rebecca stumbled away to find her husband, still chuckling as she rounded the corner to the living room.

I did the same, yet made sure to keep my steps straight and head held high.

Once I reached Carl's side, I dug my nails into his forearm with enough force to draw blood. "Honey, would you please come help me get some more wine from the garage? We're almost out."

"Oh, sure thing, sweetie," Carl muttered, startled at my interruption and, probably, the pain in his arm. "Coco was just offering her condolences, weren't you?"

The biggest blue eyes I'd ever seen in person stared blankly at me. Maybe the doctor removed some of her brain matter and used it to overstuff her tits? That would explain the vacant, vapid look on her face. Her eyes were framed by at least two sets of false eyelashes, making her look like a real Barbie. The urge to rip them off and shove them down her throat until she choked hit me.

Hard.

"I'm so sorry about Renee. You must be devastated," Coco said in a breathy whisper.

What the fuck? The girl sounded like she was channeling Marilyn Monroe. Any second, she'd break out into "Happy birthday, Mr. President."

"Rachel," I hissed through clenched teeth, a forced smile on my face. "And yes, I am. Please tell your mother we appreciate the apple pie."

"Thank you! I made it all by myself! Mom says the way to a man's heart is through his—"

"Excuse us, please," I replied, giving Carl's arm a yank, pulling him away before Blow-Up Barbie finished her sentence. "I need my husband's help."

Coco smiled, revealing a set of teeth so white they looked like painted Chiclets. She turned and strutted down the hallway toward the living room. The sway of her hips hypnotized every male over the age of six in the room, and infuriated the females stuck watching their men's tongues hit the floor.

"Okay, you can remove your claws from my arm," Carl mumbled.

Rather than heading to the garage, I took a detour and pushed him into the guest bathroom. After shutting the door and turning on the overhead fan, I let him have it.

"Are you insane? You do realize she's underage, right? If you try and play around with that piece of plastic, you'll end up in jail. Think about how that would devastate our daughter! That little bitch-in-heat is *younger* than our daughter! How would you feel if some of your friends drooled over Carol like that? Huh?"

"Ah, honey, calm down. I was just talking to the girl. She's really quite nice. Besides, I've only got eyes for you, Roxanne. Come on, let's play around. I've read that funerals are a great time to have sex. The best way to deal with death is by doing something to make you feel alive."

Carl broke out into his favorite song, one that was cute the first 100 times I'd heard it. After the first 1,000, it ceased to be funny, especially since Carl sang it every single time he was *in the mood.*

"Roxanne, you don't have to—"

Carl never finished his awful rendition of the song made

famous by The Police. I ended the tune, and his amorous intentions, by knocking the wind from his lungs after balling up my fist and punching him right in his bulging watermelon. "Lay off the bourbon, Carl. Today is the day to mourn my sister, not attempt to put your dick into jailbait, or me, for that matter. Jesus, you're pathetic."

I left my husband gasping for air in the bathroom, returning to the solemn festivities. After all, one must play the proper hostess no matter what mishaps occur, right? Anger made it impossible to recall which Rule Number that was, but I knew it was one of them, and I'm a suburban housewife—I am supposed to follow the rules.

The question burning inside my mind of how much longer I'd let the rules govern my thoughts, attitude, and actions, made a wicked grin appear. Allowing myself a bit of release—first with Benny and now with Carl—was intoxicating. As I re-entered the kitchen, I put the mask of serenity back in place, almost a bit frightened from glimpsing my inner monster twice in one day.

Almost.

It was after 8 p.m. by the time the final, drunken guests staggered out the front door. Liz and Rebecca stayed, helping me clean up the kitchen. Per the usual nightly ritual, Carl locked himself in the study. I wondered how many times he'd get it up while imagining Coco Shock sprawled out naked, firm, giant ass up in the air, taking it like a champ up the ol' wazoo. Considering how much bourbon he'd tossed back, he should be passed out, balls emptied, sleeping like a baby the rest of the night on the couch.

God help the man if he tried to put the moves on me again. The evening might just end with a man's balls getting sliced off after all!

Demerit for me for bypassing Rule Number Ten.

Do I care? Not in the slightest.

Carol surprised me by helping clean up too. The girl who

spawned countless arguments about the deplorable state of her bedroom, never once lifting a finger to help me keep the 5,000 square feet of house clean, worked by my side the entire two hours it took to return the home to normal. She even put down her favorite toy—a small pile of plastic and metal known as a cell phone, which never happened—and showed sincere interest in tidying our destroyed home.

Thank goodness, because L.B. didn't do much at all other than polish off another bottle of wine and eat leftovers. A few times, she snapped pictures of several floral arrangements then fiddled with her phone. I assumed she was tweeting or posting the images to some silly social media site. L.B. was *obsessed* with making sure everyone knew what she was doing at all times.

The fascination by vapid, self-centered, and superficial fools like Rebecca, who assumed their pathetic lives needed to be shared with the world, made me wonder about where our society was headed. I get the need to have relationships with others—it's an inborn human trait for people to congregate, from small family groups to neighborhoods, cities, states, and ultimately countries. But with the invention of the digital age came the loss of the real art of communication: Looking someone in the eye while talking, watching, and hearing the inflections in their voice or the emotions on their faces; the joy of going to the mailbox and discovering someone had taken the time to handwrite a note or send a card was yet another thing of the past I missed. Colorful emoticons inserted next to a sentence didn't possess the ability to convey the real meaning or thoughts behind characters strung together to make words.

I steered clear of the whole digital age, much to the dismay of my daughter, L.B., and even my friends. I didn't care if they considered me some weird, old-school dinosaur. I wouldn't risk putting something into the superhighway that would come back to haunt me later.

I kept my eye on Rebecca while she tapped the keys on her

cell, ready to pounce if she dared move her hands anywhere near my beloved Moscato.

"Are you going to visit Grandma tomorrow?" Carol asked after putting the last of the silverware away. "If so, may I come too? I know she doesn't understand Aunt Rachel's gone, but I do, and I feel sort of bad she didn't come to the service today to say goodbye."

I damn near dropped the vase of flowers in my hands. Wow, how much wine had I downed? Enough, obviously, I was hallucinating. Carol hated the memory care facility Mom lived in. The few times she'd accompanied me before, all she did was complain about the smell and how Grandma thought she was an old friend from high school rather than her granddaughter.

"We aren't going to see Grandma tomorrow," Rebecca piped up, words so slurred it was difficult to understand them. "It's too soon after losing Rachel. Your mom and I can't handle that much sadness in twenty-four hours. We'll go next Friday. Grandma isn't coherent enough to realize we missed a week."

Carol's pale face scrunched in disgust. "I can't go next Friday, Aunt Becca. It's freshman orientation at college."

Annoyed by Rebecca's audacity to speak for me, I added: "If you want to go see Grandma, I'll take you. She won't remember our visit, or even who we are, but that doesn't matter. We'll know."

Liz set the dish towel on the counter then walked over and put her arm around my shoulder. "I haven't seen your mom in weeks. I've just been wrapped up with helping Richard study for finals. How about I take Carol, and you rest? This has been a difficult time for you, and I need to add some credits to my friend jar. Okay?"

Leaning my head against Liz's shoulder, I sighed. My God but did she smell good. The expensive perfume was heavenly. "I don't know how I'd survive without you, Liz. You keep being so wonderful, and soon, I'll move you from number two to one on my list of favorite things, beating out Moscato."

Carol bristled, crinkling her pert nose. "Hey! Where do I rank? It sounds to me like I'm third, right behind booze and a best friend."

"I know, I didn't even make the top ten," Rebecca slurred.

Wrong, L.B. You're number one on my list—the list of people I hate.

Turning my gaze to my beautiful daughter, I almost popped out a rude comment. I stopped short when I noticed genuine sadness behind her eyes, wishing I could open my mouth and suck the words back in. "Oh, honey, you're on a list all alone. It's called my reason for living list."

Picking up her phone from the counter, Carol did something she hadn't in a long time: She smiled. "Nice save, Mom. I'm going to meet Cheri and Ellen to go over Cheri's college applications, okay? I'll be back before midnight. Promise."

Nodding, I leaned over and hugged Carol's neck. Though she wore designer perfume, she still retained the scent of my child, imprinted the moment I held her for the first time. "Thanks for all your help, sweetheart. Not another minute after midnight."

Carol returned the hug then disappeared down the hall. In seconds, the front door slammed and she was gone.

Rebecca stood and almost fell over. She caught herself, snapping off two fake nails, cussing a blue streak. "Dammit! I just had them done!"

"Rebecca, let me drive you home. I'm heading out too. Roxy needs to rest."

Waving her bloody fingers in the air, Rebecca dismissed Liz's words, flinging droplets of blood all over my clean kitchen. I contemplated grabbing her by the head and using her fake hair to soak it up.

"I live one block away. I'm fine," Rebecca responded with her usual nasty tone.

"No, you aren't. I insist," Liz replied, snagging Rebecca's purse from the counter. "Roxy doesn't need to bail you out of jail or plan another funeral for a sister. No arguments."

Stifling a laugh, I smiled while Liz lured Rebecca to follow her by jangling the keys to the SUV in front of her face. My twatwaffle, wealthy sister looked like a dog on an invisible leash. Better yet, the way she stumbled over her feet almost made her look like a shuffling zombie. Dammit! Where's my camera? This would be a perfect chance to snap an unflattering picture to hold over her head for years.

"And this one here, children? That's your great-aunt Becca, so drunk she could hardly stand. Yes, she's the same one I told you about before—the one whose nose literally fell apart after snorting cocaine! Remember, kiddies, don't drink or do drugs!"

God, why did it have to be Rachel who died? Why?

When the door closed and the SUV roared to life, exhaustion slammed into me so hard I considered curling up into a ball on the kitchen floor.

Instead, I grabbed a bottle of Moscato, bypassing Carl's study without a second glance, and headed out to the pool. Once I reached the hot tub, I turned on the jets, shed my clothes (Rule Number—oh, hell, I'm too trashed to remember the number. No matter. We nailed the rule for having an eight-foot privacy fence surrounding our lush backyard so nosy neighbors are barred from seeing our nighttime shenanigans). After pouring a full glass, I slid into the warm bubbles, letting frothy water soothe my sore muscles.

Roxy's New Rule Number One: Always maintain a constant supply of wine and the jets on at full blast to keep from going insane.

Nailed it!

The hot water and the additional wine helped ease the turbulence inside my heart. After the third glass, the wetness on my face wasn't from the steam.

I cried for the loss of Rachel. Dad. Mom (even though she's still breathing, her mind is gone, same as being dead) and how angry I am at the world. An entire life spent pursuing the American Dream, trying to do the right thing, and look where I landed? Mourning the loss of my favorite sister; drunk in a hot tub; a child heading off to college, leaving me alone with a porn-addicted spouse; a remaining sibling I hate; a mother who doesn't even know her own name, and a wasted life.

"Want some company?"

Carl's voice in the dark made me spill my wine, which pissed me off. Only one full glass remained inside the bottle. "You scared me!"

Naked as the day he was born (just with a bigger gut), glass of bourbon in one hand, a stogie in the other, Carl slipped into the seat next to me. "Sorry. I thought you heard me walk out here."

I considered a smart retort, but the part of my brain in charge of witty comebacks was soaked with too much wine.

"I'm sorry about earlier, babe. Really."

"Sorry for trying to bang me in the bathroom or practically dry-humping Coco in the hallway?"

Oh! Guess the witty retort section sparked to life for a brief second.

"I wasn't trying to upset you. Believe it or not, I was trying to make you feel better. I know how much you loved Rachel and how much responsibility you've shouldered during the last two weeks. I just, I don't know. Ever since you got the call from the hospital Rachel was sick, you've changed. You disrupted the service by making Benny leave, which isn't like you. And that little display of anger in the bathroom and your new smart mouth? All the years we've known each other, you've never, ever, been a violent person or said such rude things. I'm concerned about you."

I snorted. "Hmmm. Guess alcohol and grief don't mix well."

Carl stared up at the stars, puffing away on the cigar. The smell made me want to vomit. If my hand-eye coordination was better, I'd reach over and stuff the expensive Cuban down his throat. Let him see what it's like having something hard forced down the ol' windpipe.

Instead of making my husband experience a blowjob with a

cigar, I kept my hands busy by gulping down the remainder of my wine. He was right, though I certainly wouldn't give him the satisfaction of agreeing with what he'd said. Sick, warped thoughts about others had remained inside my head for over forty years. I put on the serene face and polite act I was taught from an early age, keeping my ugly, hateful thoughts to myself and enjoying them when they took over my dreams.

Until today.

Oops. If I didn't watch myself, my demerit jar would overflow.

Carl interrupted my maniacal thoughts. "The last few years have been stressful for you, Roxy. Carol grew up, which ended the role of room mother and taxi service. Your dad passed away. Then Claire went downhill and we had to put her in a memory care facility."

"We?" I countered. "I don't recall you helping, or anyone else for that matter."

Sighing in frustration, Carl continued. "Carol's leaving the nest, and now losing Rachel. Maybe you should go see a therapist or something? Work through the angst?"

"I'm not crazy, Carl."

"I never said you were. Oh, who am I kidding? After all of the drama you've endured with your mother, you and doctors mesh like water and oil. How about getting a job, or going back to school? Like Rebecca, you've always been good with numbers. You kept us on a tight budget; scrimped and saved money; paid the bills. Insisted the majority of the money my parents left us went into savings rather than extravagant purchases."

"Not all of it. I lost the battle when you bought that stupid Mercedes."

Carl rolled his eyes. "Stop interrupting me, Roxy. Find something, *anything*, to focus your energies into, rather than drinking yourself into an early grave. You've been hitting the wine more than normal—which is understandable considering all that's happened—but it's starting to affect your memory."

"Excuse me? What the hell does that mean? My memory is just fine."

What I wanted to say was I'd give up wine if he gave up porn. Neither was among the realm of possibilities for either of us.

"Really? I beg to differ. You've missed appointments from neglecting to put them on your calendar; forgot to pay a few bills on time. Things like that. Oh, and last week, you spent three hours looking for your cell phone and Carol found it in the fridge!"

Annoyed, yet not really in the mood for an epic battle of wits (which of course, I'd win) I said: "There's been a lot on my plate, Carl. Cut me some slack, will you? Don't you feel the slightest hypocritical for chastising me about drinking too much? I'm the one who goes to the liquor store. I know how much bourbon you drink."

Furrowing his brow, Carl stared at the bubbles in the hot tub. "All this has been hard on me too, Roxy. Watching you go through all this pain hurts me. I'm really worried about you. I don't want to lose you. I think that's what sent your father into cardiac arrest—he couldn't handle watching Claire lose her mind. I certainly couldn't handle the devastation of you looking at me without having a clue who I was. It would break me. You've always been my rock."

The words were genuine. I heard the heavy sentiment in Carl's voice. Looking over, the aqua-colored lights from the hot tub made Carl's face look younger. Concern, and was that—holy cow, there it was—the look of love, danced across his face.

I didn't tell my husband he was right about sex and funerals with words, I showed him with my body.

Looked like I'd gain back the demerit for dismissing Rule Number Ten earlier, though I wasn't about to ride the pony for Carl's sake.

It was all about me.

CHAPTER 3

I'm Supposed To Handle This How?

After Carl and Carol left to start their busy days, I stood in the kitchen, staring at the coffeemaker. My head thumped in time with the impatient foot taps as I waited for the liquid gold to brew. Between the stress, an untold amount of wine, and a night humping like a teenager in the hot tub, I needed an entire pot to set me straight and vanquish the disturbing thought patterns from yesterday. Rather than dwell on the fact my inner beast had roared to life, I decided to chalk up the violent imagery as a by-product of my grief. No blood and gore for this demure housewife! Nope, those yearnings needed to stay inside my demented dreams. I would, however, take serious stock of some other areas of my life.

It certainly was time.

Fridays were earmarked for mopping the floors, dusting, and cleaning the pool. For over fifteen years, I'd adhered to the strict schedule I set up, only deviating when I was sick or one of Carol's school activities popped up. Every other day of the week had a list of items to check off, and I stuck to them like superglue on fingers. Just because I didn't work "outside the home" didn't mean

I wasn't organized! Taking cues from my mother, Rule Number Fifteen about maintaining a tidy home was a snap.

Ever since my taxi days ended after Carol got her license, I started a new tradition. I gave myself forty minutes of me time each morning after the hubster and offspring departed. I'd enjoy several stout cups of coffee, smoke like a freight train on the back deck, and read. Once finished, I'd head inside and hit the weights and treadmill in our home gym. The extra bedroom had been earmarked for another child but, again, uncooperative reproductive organs changed the plans. I'd spend an hour each morning to rid myself of the poison I'd consumed the previous day.

After bypassing the dreaded 40 it took a lot more effort to maintain a nice figure. Unlike several of my neighbors, who were too lazy or pampered to sweat, I refused to keep up my looks by visiting a doctor and have he or she whack, slice, or inject shit, to stay young.

Nope! One trip to the plastic surgeon for breast reduction was all I needed, thank you very much. No knives, needles, or chemical alterations will touch this body!

Rule Number Fifty-three: A suburban housewife must maintain a pleasing appearance for her spouse at all times, no matter what.

Score one for me; a huge demerit for Elaine Shock.

Today was different. I'd finished the erotic romance already and couldn't quite remember which novel was next on the reading list for book club. If my headache would ease up just a tad, I could go look for the list, but meh, why? Sasha was on a romance kick, and if I read another sappy, *Oh, baby, I love you so much I'll show you by giving up everything to prove it* novel, I'd puke.

Literally.

Toss up my cookies all over my clean floor. Romances were nothing but trash and drivel and completely unrealistic. I didn't know one single couple who married because of true love, not even my parents. They married because they were supposed to—again, sticking to the rules—not because they couldn't stand being apart from each other. Of course, that little bundle of truth I didn't discover until Mom's mind deteriorated and I put her into the memory care facility. While going through all her belongings, packing, sorting, and crying like a lost goat, I discovered the truth about the sham marriage of Roger and Claire Rayburn: Pregnancy.

Hmmm. Like mother, like daughter. Wonder if a sinus infection fucked-up her life too?

Demerit!

The *real* marriage certificate, with a date only three months before I burst from the womb, had been stuffed in the back of Mom's closet, buried underneath piles of paper. I laughed and cried at the same time, realizing all the massive anniversary parties thrown for Mr. and Mrs. Roger Rayburn had been off by six months.

No, I wouldn't think about the dream marriage I'd always looked up to and strove to emulate. Knowing the union of Roger and Claire Rayburn was faker than Rebecca's new tits made me feel nauseated. I'd already dealt with that load of emotional garbage anyway, months ago.

"That's enough, Roxy. It's time to refocus and stop thinking about the ugly truth behind the shiny façades everyone wears. Back to book club woes!" I muttered while pouring a full cup of black gold.

We'd kicked up the heat level several notches last month at the request of Sasha. The latest erotic bestseller destroyed countless brain cells after reading. Gag. Gag. Double gag. Yes, a woman's lonely, fucked-up life can be fixed by a man with bulging biceps, abs and chest tight enough to bounce quarters from and slipping his *enormous* schlong inside every available orifice.

Same is true for the uber-wealthy, emotionally damaged billionaire playboys: The right pussy to control would save them from a lifetime of sorrow and loneliness.

Please. Orgasms are great but they certainly aren't life-altering!

The next time our group of bored housewives converged at

Sasha's, I planned on lobbying for a thriller, one full of psychotic deviants wreaking havoc on unsuspecting victims, rather than the next book on the agenda. I'm sure it will be yet another literary masterpiece entitled *The Perils of Pussy* or *Adventures of the Perilous Penis* or something equally gross. Yeah, I was ready for something dark, sinister, and full of gore.

Oops. Another demerit.

Rule Number Thirty-seven: Housewives must always maintain a happy, well-adjusted demeanor, a perpetual smile on their faces, even when sad or disgusted.

Seriously, who cares about the freaking rules? Didn't I decide yesterday to make my own, anyway? *The Suburbia Handbook* was grossly outdated and in desperate need of an overhaul. I was a dying breed, and it was time to start *Roxy's Rules for Living.*

By nature, I was a note taker. I wrote down everything from detailed grocery lists, family schedules, vacation itineraries, you name it. My OCD drove Carol to the brink of insanity when she was applying for scholarships. In the end, she gave up and opted to take the free ride offered from Carl's university (another perk of being a tenured professor!) not because Carol wanted to go to college so close to home, but because she couldn't take another tenpage list of notes from me.

Since I was sober, Carl's ridiculous suggestions prior to our hot tub encounter drummed inside my head. The man had some nerve to suggest I see a shrink or that I was losing my memory like Mom! Hello pot, I'm kettle—have you considered plopping on the psychiatrist's couch to discuss your own issues? No, I'm sure the great Professor Davenport wouldn't dream of baring his soul to a stranger then hearing the words: "Sir, I believe you have an unhealthy addiction to pornography. We need to work on that issue."

Getting a job was out of the question. Seriously, what the hell would I do? Two years of college spent taking general classes (because I was too busy partying and going to football games to watch the once hunk of a man play ball—then got knocked up) wouldn't help me in the least.

I had no discernible skills to speak of, so what could I do, realistically? Sling java down at the local coffee shop to my snobby neighbors as they rushed off to work? The only enjoyment there would be me spitting in their double latte skim mochas. Work the counter at some superstore? Greet strangers with a fake smile while urging them to enjoy their day? Biting my tongue each time I wanted to say something snarky, like: "Thanks for choosing to shop with us! I hope you enjoy your shopping experience of purchasing cheap shit that will last all of five minutes. Get your crap, go home, and then attempt to pass it off as expensive purchases to all your friends and neighbors."

Thank you, but I'll pass.

No, instead of giving my spouse the satisfaction that he'd offered up viable solutions to my problems, I'd fix the hole inside my chest all by myself. Today, I would start a new tradition—actually writing down my new life rules, rather than adhering to the non-existent, antiquated set embedded inside my mind. Trudging back inside, head still pounding, I snatched a notebook from the junk drawer and headed back to the deck. Pen at the ready, it took me a few seconds to remember the first rule I'd come up with last night. Wine, it had something to do with wine. Ah, yes:

Roxy's New Rule Number One: Always maintain a constant supply of wine and the jets on at full blast to keep from going insane.

A sense of giddiness after writing down the first rule made me smile, despite my throbbing head. It didn't take long for me to come up with the second item.

Roxy's New Rule Number Two: Mentally incinerate The Suburbia Handbook and move into the twenty-first century like every other woman has done!

Oh, I'm on a roll! This is liberating! Hmm, did the new ideas spring forth after last night's sexual release in the water?

Possibly, though it certainly wasn't because of Carl's great moves. While doing the nasty in the hot tub, I closed my eyes and pretended I was riding Tom Selleck, cowboy hat and chaps still on, rather than my bland husband. Did I feel guilty about this switch of identities? Absolutely not! There was no doubt in my hungover mind Carl was picturing himself thrusting his cock into Coco, so we were even. I got my rocks off while grinding on *Quigley Down Under* while Carl blew his wad by porking Blow-Up Barbie.

Roxy's New Rule Number Three: To achieve multiple, mind-blowing orgasms, picture Matthew Quigley. Check! Ride 'em cowboy!

Satisfied with my progress, I lit a smoke while enjoying my coffee. More new rules bounced about inside my head, each one more disturbing and twisted than the one before. My dark fantasies were interrupted by Rebecca's assigned ringtone on my phone: Lunatic Fringe, er, Bitch.

"How's the head?"

"Pounding," Rebecca whined. "That cheap wine you served did a number on me."

"Alcohol is alcohol. Drink too much, no matter how expensive, you suffer the next day."

"Whatever. Listen, though I enjoy our little verbal sparring matches, I didn't call to discuss my hangover."

"Okay, so why did you?"

Rebecca huffed. "I told you we need to talk about the trust and Mom's house. We don't have much time to make the changes before Stephen and I are liable for the taxes."

"God, you are a vicious wench. Your life revolves around money. Rachel hasn't even been in the ground a day and you're already—"

"Roxy, it has to be addressed! I'm the next in line for the house."

"Yes, I'm well aware of that. Recall I'm the one who went with Mom to get all her affairs in order before she forgot who she was? I specifically put myself last in line because I was trying to be fair to you and Rachel."

"Oh, how sweet. A moment of kindness from the great Roxy! Don't try and play off that you did it for any reason other than you wanted another feather to add to your hat."

"Goodness, sister, what a low opinion you have of me. I'm so hurt," I responded, a devious grin on my face. "Shouldn't we try to make amends, bury the sisterly hatchet now that it's just the two of us?"

Rebecca snorted. "Please. We're way beyond that, Roxy, so stay on topic, please. I explained to you a hundred times while Rach was in the hospital why we don't want the house. It's not that we can't afford it we just don't need the tax liability! We already have four rent houses, and I don't want the hassle of handling another. I've had our lawyer draw up the papers, passing ownership over to you. What you do with Mom's house after it's transferred to you is not my business. And who knows? You might just need the place soon."

"What the hell does that mean?"

"It means, dear sister," Rebecca responded, softening her tone, "with Carol leaving, you'll need something to occupy your time. Being a landlord is full of all sorts of activities. Collecting the rent, maintaining the residence—"

"Enough. I get it. Sheesh, you're just as bad as Carl. I got an earful last night about what I should do with my life now that things are changing. Fine. You win. What do I need to do?"

"Nothing except sign on the dotted line. I'll have a courier drop the papers off this afternoon."

"A courier? That's silly and beyond pretentious! You live around the freaking corner! Just bring them by after work."

"Unlike you, Roxy, I have a very full life and little time to spare. That's why God invented young men who enjoy wearing tight bicycle shorts. I'll make sure to request one who has the thighs of a Greek God."

Yes, my sister is a bitch, but sometimes, she is hysterical. "Make sure to ask for one with no body hair, okay? I can't stomach a man-beast. I'll be home all day."

"Well duh, what else would you be doing? Your nails since you're too cheap to get them done professionally? Slaving over a hot stove cooking some meal that no one will appreciate? Wait, I know! Not a damn thing except cleaning."

"If Mom heard us—or anyone else for that matter—talking to each other with such disrespect and ugliness, our fake personas would disappear. You know, up until today, I didn't really grasp how odd our relationship is."

"Can't pull the wool over the eyes of the people who know the real you," Rebecca answered, her voice dripping with sarcasm. "We've had each other's numbers since childhood. I don't recall there being a law or rule somewhere that said one must love or even like a blood relative."

"Neither do I. Good thing we get to choose our friends."

"No doubt, which is why I didn't pick you. I mean, how could I? You waste so much of your time doing things you could pay another to do it's ridiculous. We have nothing in common except DNA."

"Bitch. Actually, I'm busy plotting out some new directions for my life, thank you very much. Bye."

Ending the call before Rebecca had a chance to say a word, I decided to head upstairs and take a long, hot shower. I didn't like the idea of taking over ownership of our childhood home for a variety of reasons, but at least I would make sure it was well taken care of.

"Dammit, Rachel! You shouldn't be dead. You should be here, minus Benny-Boo, living in the same neighborhood, chasing little replicas of yourself around the yard. Mom wanted you to live there, and now, you never will. Some stranger will be roaming around in our old rooms, defiling our memories!"

I made it to the top of the stairs when the doorbell rang. Great!

I'm still in my tattered robe with no makeup on. Rebecca must have already called the courier service before she contacted me, knowing they'd show up and I'd look like yesterday's trash.

Bitch!

The doorbell chimed again, so instead of rushing to change clothes, I went back downstairs. The courier was probably close to jailbait age, so there was no need to primp and preen. The Davenport household didn't need another sexual predator roaming the rooms.

To my surprise, a courier with a cute helmet and sexy legs wasn't standing on my stoop. Instead, I was greeted by a girl, maybe twenty, with long, blonde hair, entirely too much makeup, and a worried look on her face. Clutched in her left hand was a Manila folder.

"May I help you?" I asked, assuming she was lost. She certainly wasn't a Jehovah's Witness. They didn't wear designer jeans, makeup, fake fingernails, or high heels.

"Uh, yes. I'm looking for Professor Davenport. Is he here?"

"No, he's at school."

An eerie sensation tickled the back of my mind. Though a rarity, a few students over the years dropped by unannounced, usually to beg for a better grade, chance to retake a test, or other such nonsense.

The eeriness morphed into nausea when the girl's hand rubbed her stomach.

Her pregnant stomach.

"Are you, oh, God. You aren't the maid, are you?"

Unable to form words, I shook my head. What a stupid question! How many maids worked in their robes? Answer—zero. The girl's IQ probably hovered close to the size of her bra.

It hit me then—she was just Carl's type. I wouldn't be surprised if her name was Dior since she looked like Coco's older sister.

Hmm, what is that sensation inside my chest and the weird, cracking noise filling my head? Was it possible I just experienced my heart breaking? If so, does that mean a part of me still loved the man who used to snuggle next to me years ago, stroking my hair, whispering his love? The other 50 per cent of Carol's genetic pool, who enjoyed sneaking up behind me, cupping my breasts and cooing, "Oh, I wish I could be your bra for just one day." The same man who looked genuinely sad less than one day ago as he professed he was worried about me?

How about that? There was still a spark of love for Carl. Of course, the key word in that thought: *Was*.

Oh! Another unfamiliar sound! Could it be? Why yes, yes it was—the *snap* of the last thin tendril holding my sanity in place.

Something inside my mind broke loose at the realization my husband's dick had played around inside the girl's vaggie-shack. Though the chances to do so had been plenty, including one awkward, drunken encounter when Mr. Shock happened upon me *sans clothes* in the hot tub years ago, I'd never, not once, betrayed our vows. Oh, I sometimes fantasized about other men while my legs were up in the air, but I never acted upon them.

Obviously, the whores onscreen weren't enough for Carl and he sought out a real, live fuck-buddy. I was beyond livid yet calm at the same time, just like I recalled my mother acting when angry. The Rayburn clan never worried when she yelled—it was when her voice became a sugary-sweet mixture while her jaw was set tight that sent us all scattering.

It was a terrifying combination—not for me, but for the pregnant hot pepper standing on my stoop.

Tears burst from the girl's wide, green eyes. "His wife, then? Carl's married? I'm so sorry! He didn't tell me—oh, shit. What am I going to do now?"

"May I assume you're holding paternity papers?" I asked, my voice sweeter than raw honey while I marveled at the fact Carl's little swimmers still held some power. Stroke! Stroke!

"Yes. The results just came back today. I flipped out at work, so my boss told me to leave. I, oh, forgive me. I shouldn't be talking about this with you, Mrs. Davenport. And I am sorry. Again, I didn't know Carl had a wife."

Pulling from reserves I wasn't aware I possessed, I asked: "What's your name?"

"Ginger. Ginger Holloway. God, I don't know what I'm going to do!" Ginger sobbed.

Ginger! Oh, that's even better than Dior! The girl is a spicy condiment. The Habanero hot sauce poured over my milk-toast life. Fire, fire, *fire*!

"I can't raise a baby alone. I've got two more years of school! I'm so sorry, Mrs. Davenport, but he's going to have to take financial responsibility."

Oh, you won't raise it alone, Hottie Habanero. You'll have your baby daddy to help, because in about thirty seconds, once my brain fully processes this nightmare, I'm calling a lawyer.

Good thing I already made the decision to burn the *Handbook*, because I was on the cusp of dumping a huge pile of demerits onto my head by breaking Rule Number Fifty:

Once the vows are said, married couples must remain together until death do they part.

Screw that.

Roxy's New Rule Number Four: When your husband knocks up a walking condiment because he neglected to use a condom, it broke, or again, a fucking sinus infection derails your life plans, you divorce his sorry, cheating ass, and take him to the cleaners. If that doesn't work out the way intended, end the marriage by death.

Double. Fucking. Check.

Rule Number Ninety-three: A housewife must always maintain her composure, even under the direst of circumstances.

Must obey this old rule from the *Handbook* or I'll lunge from the doorway and kill this little bitch with my bare hands.

Taking a deep breath, I purred, "No need to apologize, Ms. Holloway. Your life isn't the first one he's ruined because of unsafe sex. I'll make sure to tell him the happy news about his impending fatherhood, and then I'm sure he'll contact you. Hope you have room for him to stay with you, because he just lost a place to live. Given your current predicament, I assume he knows the way to your bedroom?"

Ginger nodded through her tears. Streaks of black mascara cascaded down her cheeks. Obviously, the girl wasn't raised properly and didn't understand the importance of waterproof mascara. Fumbling around with the folder, she extracted a piece of paper and handed it to me, gave me one last, embarrassed look and then tottered down the sidewalk.

I slammed the door and locked it. Leaning against the heavy wood for support, I took a deep breath and scanned the paper. Sure enough, it was the results of a DNA test: Carl Andrew Davenport listed under father.

Carl's initials fit the situation.

Anger roared from deep within, consuming all rational thought. In a fit of rage, I stormed into the dining area and hurled the crystal vase Carl's mother bought us as a wedding gift across the room. I laughed like a demented hyena as it shattered into hundreds of tiny shards after connecting with the wall.

The thought of telling Carol the wretched news made my stomach revolt. I barely made it to the kitchen sink before tossing up last night's wine and this morning's coffee. While puking into the beautiful, stainless steel sink, my thoughts were a jumbled mess.

Carl's going to pay, dearly, for destroying my life.

Carol's.

Our future grandchildren.

Ruining our family's reputation that I worked my entire life to keep at a high standard.

Disturbing images of holiday events filled my mind. Carl showing up with a walker; Hottie Habanero bouncing and jiggling while chasing their child around the dinner table, the unplanned fruit of his loins *playing and eating right next to Carol's children*, made my vision blur.

No. Way.

The vow I made at Rachel's funeral burst inside my head—kill whoever had the balls to attempt to destroy my family. I didn't leave a loophole for family members, so Carl wouldn't get a reprieve. Fuming, I paced in small circles, hands balled into tight fists, skin prickling as dark fury pumped through my body while imagining what sick, twisted ways I could off my husband and pin his death on Hottie Habanero.

No, I wouldn't kill Carl, though I might just castrate him. Turn him from stallion to gelding with one quick slice. He'd be like one of the neutered cats Rachel brought home years ago: Fat, slow, spending his remaining days on earth sitting in the window-sill, staring outside with dull, lifeless eyes.

Yes, that's your punishment C.A.D. If I actually end up killing someone, it will be the knocked-up whore, because I'll do whatever necessary to protect my daughter from having to deal with your indiscretion.

Whatever. It. Takes.

Divorce or death?

Oh, who am I kidding? I'm not capable of *killing* someone, or even cutting off body parts. A few punches, yes, but that's it. I may *think* the thoughts, yet *acting* upon them is an entirely different set of skills I don't possess. Hell, I gag when preparing raw chicken. Even if I could release my rage, the consequences would be devastating for my little girl. No, I wouldn't let Carol be stuck the remainder of her life with the stigma of *My Mom Was a Killer.* That label would be worse than *My Dad's a Whoredog and My Step-mom's My Age!*

Decision made, I shoved the nail in Carl's coffin into my pocket and headed straight to my phone in the kitchen. My fingers shook so hard I had to use voice commands to call the meanest, ugliest, down-and-dirty person I knew: L.B.

She answered on the second ring. "I'm swamped, what's up?"

"Rebecca, I need a lawyer. Shark of all sharks. The kind who'd eat their offspring for a dollar."

"What? Why? I told you we had our lawyer draw up the deed transfer. I'm your sister, for Godsakes. Don't you trust me? It's solid, I—"

"Not for that, you idiot. I need a divorce lawyer. Who's the best in town?"

Rebecca gasped. "Divorce? Roxy, what's wrong?"

My touch with sanity, which had been hanging on with just one, thin tendril, snapped. "I didn't call to talk to you about it! I called to get the name of a lawyer. Apparently, I have a life now, too, and don't have time to spare, either. I don't plan on rehashing the worst moment of my life, one on a par with burying our sister less than fifteen hours ago and putting Mom in a home! Name and number, or I swear, I'll come apart at the fucking seams and kill the next person I see."

"Breathe, Roxy. Breathe. The best lawyer in town is Reginald Greenwood. After Chad Shelnut got caught humping his assistant in the parking lot of his building, Reginald got Maxine Shelnut the house, alimony, half of Chad's retirement—"

"Number," I hissed.

"I'll text it to you. Give me five."

"Three's all you got."

"Roxy, I'm so sorry."

I hung up before anymore fake concern spewed from Rebecca's lips. Looking at the mess I'd made, the housewife in me urged the body to clean it up. The mind of the pissed off wife said fuck it. In the end, old habits won out. I didn't want Carol to come home and see the mess and start asking questions I wasn't prepared to answer yet.

Same held true for Carl. It was among the realms of possibilities he'd already received a phone call: A very distraught phone call from Hottie, full of tears and accusations. Maybe the adultery gods would take pity on me and Carl would suffer a massive heart attack after hearing the joyous news!

My phone chimed, signaling a text from Rebecca.

Divorce—here we come. God, Carol, I'm so sorry, but I can't, I *won't*, stay with your father. Not when another woman is carrying his child. I can't. I simply can't.

Demerit. Demerit. Fucking demerit.

"Glad your mind is gone, Mom, because if it wasn't already, a dead daughter and a divorced one would have surely pushed you over the edge. Sorry. I tried to follow your rules, but a younger, big-chested hot pepper stole the show."

Clicking on the text from Rebecca, I jotted the number down on the notepad. Thoughts raced inside my head at breakneck speed. Okay, I need to breathe. Think. Carol's shift at the vet's office ended at three. Liz said she'd take her to see Mom. That gave me until about five or six to plan.

Carl. School was out, so why was he there? Ah, yes. End of semester staff meetings. Shit, all this stress turned my once sharp memory into mush. Did he know the results already? Obviously, he was aware of the possibility since he took the test. Ugh! My stomach rolled again thinking about my stupidity in the hot tub. Wooed by Carl's lies about how he loved me, deceived into having sex. Hope the bastard enjoyed the interaction because it was the last time he'd play around in my wonderland.

Was the stellar, well-known professor cowering under his desk, wondering what the hell his next move should be? Maybe he was on his way home, a handful of flowers and box of candy in tow, ready to beg for forgiveness?

Pacing the floors, mindful of the broken glass, I tried to mentally map out my next steps. The rambling thoughts were interrupted by a faint buzzing noise coming from the living room. It took me a few seconds to recognize the sound.

Aha! The soon-to-be-dad forgot his cell phone! Score!

Snatching it up from the coffee table, I laughed. He'd received six text messages and three missed calls from Hottie Habanero. No wonder she dropped by the house! She must have assumed Carl was attempting to shrug off his duties as a father and decided to confront him. Girl's got guts, no doubt.

It happened at the precise moment I scrolled through Carl's phone. My disturbing and dark plans formed in seconds, courtesy of a scene I suddenly remembered from the erotic romance book I hated so much. The novel was trash and absolute drivel on one hand, but the images it brought to life inside my demented mind would be a masterpiece once I accomplished them. Before I forgot each detail, I raced back to the deck, grabbed the notebook and jotted it all down.

Once finished, I went to the kitchen and retrieved the broom and dust pan. In the utility closet nestled on the back shelf were two cans of dog food. Beef Medley; leftovers from Ralphie, Carol's precious pooch. He'd died two years prior, and I guess I simply neglected to remove all traces of his presence inside the house.

Snatching them up, I set them on the counter, cleaned up the broken glass and then headed back out to the deck.

In a frenzy, I scribbled:

Roxy's New Rule Number Five: Every man wants the Fifty Shades of Grey *experience, right? Well, I've got a new version.* Fifty Shades of Ginger. *This titillating journey includes Carl's favorite dinner—meatloaf—with a special ingredient. Dog chow. New recipe alert! Medley Meatloaf—just add two cans—and hubby will lap it up! Optional: Give your china a nice polish by using saliva!*

Smiling, I lit a smoke then dialed Reginald Greenwood's office. To my surprise, he took my call. Score one for Rebecca!

After a twenty-minute conversation, two pages of scribble added to the notebook, I was ready to make one last phone call before I started preparing for the night's festivities.

"Liz? I need your help, please, and no questions. Okay?"

"Judging by the tone in your voice, I'd be afraid to say no. What's up?"

"I need you to occupy Carol's time tonight until at least, oh, ten p.m. Okay?"

"Occupy, as in, keeping her away from the house?" Liz hesitated, her voice full of worry.

"Yes. I'll explain later, but it's really important."

There was a long pause before Liz said: "For you, anything. However, if the cops grill me later, I don't know a thing."

Laughing, I responded: "Nothing like that, I assure you. Plan on acting out Chapter 37. Carl mentioned in passing yesterday that sex is a great way to overcome grief and I want to surprise him tonight."

"Whew, you had me going for a second there," Liz laughed. "Only on one condition."

"What?"

Lowering her voice, Liz whispered: "Promise me all the juicy details after. I've been thinking about doing the same thing to Roger. If you've got the guts to try it, and don't die in the process, I might just do it too!"

"Oh, when this night's over, I'll give you all the gory details. That's a promise. Thanks a mil, Liz. I owe you."

Hanging up, I stared at my legs, which were in desperate need of reacquainting themselves with the razor. I needed to primp and preen before the biggest night of Carl Davenport's life, but it would have to wait.

I had alterations to make to the meatloaf first. Then I could properly prepare for Operation Fifty Shades of Ginger.

It was time to release the inner monster, and my first victim would be the bastard who shared my bed while sharing another's.

CHAPTER 4

Fifty Shades Of Ginger

The last rose petal in place, all candles lit and my body clad in black lace, I waited with exceptional patience. No wine for me tonight. Nope, I needed all my wits and faculties to function at peak performance. All my attention was focused on listening for the familiar sound of Carl's Mercedes pulling into the garage. The low jazz playing throughout the house speakers vied for attention, but I ignored it. A wicked grin curved my lips upward, knowing he wouldn't be driving his favorite toy for much longer. Soon, he wouldn't be able to afford it, and he'd certainly need a bigger vehicle to tote around his growing family.

My boobs peeked out of the lace teddy, my shaven legs perched on the table, black stilettos glistening under the lights from the dimly lit chandelier and flickering candles. The rancid smell of cooked dog food finally vanquished (thanks to Mom's helpful household tip of a bowl full of vinegar) replaced with the delicious aroma of Italian meatloaf. My portion was the real deal—Carl's wasn't.

The second I heard the garage door open, my heart rate spiked with eager anticipation. That's a credit for me because housewives are supposed to be excited when their hardworking men arrive home after a busy day out in "the business sector." A quiet giggle escaped my lips. Like one measly credit would matter. It would be swallowed up by the avalanche of demerits I was about to unleash. With a final glance at the setup in front of me, making sure I hadn't forgotten anything, I smiled. I may not be a lot of things, but I was organized and capable of planning an unforgettable party!

"What the—?"

Carl's muttered comment from the front entryway almost made me laugh. The hardwood floors leading from the entrance to the dining room looked like a floral store exploded. His footsteps were hesitant as he followed the trail of doom I set up earlier.

"Hey, baby. You were so right about making love. Last night was amazing, so I decided to make your favorite dinner, and after we eat, I'm dessert. I added to the ensemble you bought me. Two sets of fuzzy handcuffs."

Carl stopped in the dining room doorway, mouth agape, gaze darting between the handcuffs on the table and my long legs draped across the edge. I'd never worn the sexy outfit he'd bought me on Valentine's Day three years ago, though he'd begged me to numerous times. Cramming my flesh inside the flimsy material had the exact effect we'd both intended. He was horny, and I felt liberated by the overwhelming sense of power thrumming inside my chest. The shock on Carl's face disappeared, replaced by lust.

Making sure my moves were slow and seductive, I rose from the chair, Long Island Tea in hand. It was a special, stout edition, laced with enough vodka to take down the Budweiser Clydesdales. Sauntering across the floor to Carl's side, I held out the drink. Crushing my body up against his, my painted red lips grazed his ear. "Have a drink while I serve you."

Carl shook with excitement, his face full of confusion and

eagerness. Looking down, I saw the bulge pressing against the seam of his slacks. Oh goody! I had him *right* where I wanted.

"God, Roxy, you look amazing. I mean, *amazing.* Handcuffs, too? I can't believe you're finally going to let me tie you up! You've always been so, I don't know, vanilla in the bedroom! Boy, I love this new, spicier version! And you said the erotic novel was boring! I knew it got you hot. I knew it!"

Making sure to roll my hips, I strutted to the kitchen, fetching our pre-made plates. I heard him take several sips of the drink, smacking his thin lips with each slurp. Before picking up the china, I pulled down one edge of the teddy, exposing my right breast. The visual would ensure Carl's attention wasn't focused on anything but my boobs. Men and mammary glands—steel to the magnet.

Yep, it worked. Carl choked, spitting tea all over my beautiful linen tablecloth. Bastard! "Eat, sweetie. You'll need the energy for later. And yes, I'm dripping wet with anticipation! I must say, it's quite exciting being so naughty. See?"

Taking Carl's hand, I guided it toward the panties, yet didn't let him touch. He shuddered with desire, trying to stick his fat, stubby sausages inside me. Backing up, I grinned and straddled the chair beside him. I stuck a red fingernail in his mashed potatoes then brought it to my lips, licking the creamy concoction with slow, long flicks of my tongue.

"Oh, Roxy, don't make me wait," Carl begged. "Carol will be home soon."

"No, she won't. I made sure of it. We've got hours, so eat and drink. I've got several things planned for tonight, which will take a lot out of us both. There's only one rule for the evening."

Swallowing the first bite of meatloaf, Carl nodded. "I promise I won't hurt you, Roxy."

That little peashooter isn't big enough to hurt a fly, you moron. Geez, all men assumed their members were the size of a horse's. "I'm not worried about that, Carl. I'm looking forward to a bit of pain. Makes a person feel alive, right? No, the rule tonight is simple: What's good for the groom is good for the bride."

Carl damn near came. A flush of red filled his cheeks. "You want to cuff me, too? Oh, God! I don't know what's gotten into you, but I'm glad it did. Yes, of course, I can't wait!"

Oh, you may not know what's gotten into me, but I assure you, husband, I know who you got into and you're going to pay dearly for dipping your wick into another candle. Smiling, I took a few bites of my untainted meatloaf while Carl gobbled his dog chow version down like, well, a dog. Smiling and nodding, listening to my spouse drone on about what he planned on doing to me in the bedroom, I kept refilling his tea while we ate. By the time we finished dinner, Carl was thoroughly buzzed.

It was time to start phase two of my devious plans. Rising to my feet, I snatched both sets of cuffs off the table. "Ready for dessert, dear?"

"Beyond," Carl answered, downing the remainder of the tea.

"Since I'm new to this experience, let me go first? It'll relax my nerves, okay? You know, vanilla needs some time to turn into hot chocolate," I purred, dangling the cuffs behind my back as I took the stairs.

"Honey, I'm your slave tonight. Do what you will."

Oh, I plan on it, baby.

***

Carl followed me upstairs. Once we reached the bedroom door, he darted past me, launching his chubby body onto the bed. I hadn't seen him move so quick since his college football days. It took him less than five seconds to shed his clothes. Seeing my husband—my fucking mate of close to twenty years—sprawled out on the bed, arms above his head, dick hard as a rock and standing at full attention, I almost laughed.

I sensed my husband wasn't a virgin when it came to bondage.

I wonder which little whore broke his cherry? There was a part of me completely dumbfounded by the fact I really didn't know my husband. Never, not even one time, had Carl ever come close to *hinting* he liked things rough.

The candles I lit earlier were the only light in the room. Pausing by the edge of the bed, I did a sexy little dance before straddling Carl's quaking thighs. Using my sweetest, childlike voice, I whispered: "I'm not sure how to do this. Do I just click them on, or—?"

Taking a pair from my hands, Carl said: "Here, like this. Now, secure the other end to the headboard, and then do the same with the other set. Do you want me to turn over so you can spank me? Did you buy a whip, too?"

Nope, my husband had his bondage cherry popped already. Demerit!

"I have several toys on the agenda for tonight, but for right now, let me play with Rufus." I ground my hips into his dick, the one I'd given the playful nickname to years ago. "Then, I'll turn you over and give your rump a good spanking. That's a promise."

"Hurry, Roxy! I'm not sure how much longer I can hold out before I cum. I want to be inside you right now!"

Cuffs finally secure, tonight's prey was now at my mercy. "Let's play a game, Carl. A Fifty Shades game."

"Yes, oh God, yes!"

Sliding down the bed, I gave Rufus a light squeeze. Closing his eyes, Carl groaned with ecstasy. It took him a second to realize I wasn't on the bed.

"Roxy? What are you—oh, shit!"

The kitchen knife looked downright terrifying under the flickering light of the candles. Smiling as I admired the sharp edges, I answered: "I said I wanted to play a game, and you agreed. It's called Fifty Shades of Ginger."

Hard dick—gone! It deflated like a popped balloon. Raging Rufus went back to Limp Biscuit. Guess Carl wasn't taking one of those blue little dick pills after all. The ones I found in the back of the closet earlier, stuffed inside the pocket of an old suit, must be old.

"Ginger?" Carl whispered, eyes bulging and face snow white.

Before Carl had a chance to move or say anything else, I jumped onto the bed, crushing his thighs under my weight. In one swift motion, I grabbed a handful of limp flesh with my left hand while bringing the sharp edge of the knife inches from the shaft with my right.

"Yep. That hot little side dish stopped by today with the joyful news! Congratulations, Professor, you're going to be a daddy, which means you'll be around sixty when the little one graduates high school. Isn't that just the neatest?"

"Oh, shit," Carl muttered.

"Those were the first words that popped into my mind when I met Ginger today! Isn't that funny? I've heard, or maybe read, somewhere, that after years of being together couples start looking and thinking alike. Obviously, the first part isn't true in our case, but it seems we're on the right track for the second! Now, we don't have time for the fifty questions I originally wanted to ask, so we'll cut them short. Oh, sorry," I giggled. "Bet *cut* isn't a word you want to hear at the moment. One circumcision is enough, huh?"

"Roxy, I—"

"You aren't playing by the rules, Carl. This is a yes or no game unless I specifically say otherwise. I want quick, honest answers or you'll get quick, harsh punishment. Ready?"

Clamping his mouth shut, Carl nodded. Though he couldn't see over his watermelon belly what I was doing, I knew he felt it. The stench of fear—along with tons of sweat—burst from his pores, making me gag.

"Before I start asking questions, remember, I've got my fingers wrapped around an organ with a vein in it. I'll be able to detect the slightest deviation in heart rate. If you lie, I'll know it. I suggest you tell the truth, even if you think it's harsh and something I might not want to hear. You ready for the first question?"

Carl nodded, a few tears leaking from the corner of his eyes.

God, this was so much fun! I am woman hear me growl!

"Good! Okay, question one: Was Ginger the first time you've been unfaithful, you know, with a real, live whore, rather than ones on the computer?"

"No," Carl mumbled.

Move over, Wonder Woman. Your lasso of truth had nothing on Raging Roxy's butcher knife and strong grip!

"First child out of wedlock?"

"Yes."

"If the test results had been negative, would you have come clean and confessed to the little", I gave the limp flesh a squeeze, "indiscretion with Ginger?"

"Yes."

I pressed the tip of the blade into his skin above the groin hard enough to hurt yet not draw blood. "Remember, honest answers, darling husband. This is your only save."

"No," Carl whimpered.

"I did a bit of research online before you arrived home. Seems paternity results can be obtained rather quickly. Now, here's a question you may answer with more than a simple yes or no: Did you give your DNA sample before or after Rachel died?"

No answer, just a weird groan.

I hummed the tune of *Jeopardy*.

Carl moaned then answered: "The day she went to the hospital."

Anger bubbled inside my chest, but I pushed it away. I needed to concentrate, keep my composure, and not succumb to rage. Carl said he was late to the hospital because he was stuck in downtown traffic. He was stuck all right—between a rock and a hard place. God, a dog bite and a whore-dog husband ruined my life *on the same fucking day!* Forcing my mind to stay calm, I took a deep breath. I had to get through the Q&A portion before I went to the bonus round. Then, I would let the fury fly.

"How many?"

"What?" Carl muttered.

"How many times have you been unfaithful during our marriage, Carl? Twice? Ten? One-hundred? Remember the rules and be honest."

Carl was crying harder now.

Glancing up, I smiled.

Tears, snot, and spittle covered his red face. "Ten."

Squeezing, I urged, "You sure?"

"Okay, okay! Ginger was the thirteenth time. But, I swear, Roxy, after the pregnancy scare, I was—"

"Uh-uh, you aren't allowed any additional comments unless I say so. And it wasn't a pregnancy scare. It's confirmed. You're having a fucking baby, at your age, with a tramp young enough to be your daughter—aren't you just a shining example to Carol?"

Carl's response was a pathetic whimper.

"Hmm, thirteen? Isn't that an unlucky number? So unlucky, in fact, buildings don't use it? Yes, I believe it is. Especially for you."

"Roxanne, please, I'm begging you. Stop. I'm so sorry."

I crushed his worthless piece of flesh between my fingers.

Carl screamed in pain, writhing underneath me.

"One more outburst like that and you'll scream so loud the entire block will hear you. Understand?"

"Yes." *Sniffle. Sniffle. Snort. Snort.*

"Okay, hang in there, honey. You're doing just fine. Let's see, what else did I want to know?" I tapped the blade against his balls.

Carl moaned in agony.

"Thirteen is quite a number. When did you first defile our vows, darling husband? Oh, and you may answer with full sentences during this line of questioning."

"After your surgery."

His answer made me laugh. A sick, twisted, maniacal laugh. Of course he did! The male attachment to big boobs left my poor husband dazed and confused, eyes gravitating to the nearest set of enormous knockers, whether real or fake. The surgery ended my physical pain yet it seemed to be the starting point for mental anguish. If Carl's number was correct, it put him close to having one affair per year since my surgery.

Bastard.

"In all your dalliances over the last *fifteen fucking years*, was this the first time you neglected to use protection?"

"Yes, well, no."

"I'm confused. Which is it?"

"I always used condoms. Always, I swear. Well, except for just once with Ginger. She caught me off guard in my office one day and—"

"That's all it takes. Just once. One moment of unbelievable weakness and look what happened? Countless lives are ruined in a flash. Oops! I'm getting sidetracked, aren't I? Bad news sometimes does that to a person. Some people don't handle life's little upheavals well. Guess I'm one of them."

"I'm sorry," Carl whined.

"I agree. You are a sorry excuse for a husband. So, here we are. The good news is, hopefully, you didn't pass any STDs to your *wife*, but that's something you can't answer. I'll leave that up to Dr. Critchon, after I see him tomorrow. I'm interested to hear the answer to my next question. What was last night in the hot tub all about? One last hurrah? A pity fuck or maybe a leftover hard-on from Coco being in the house? Remember, tell the truth."

"No."

"No to all three? Then what was the reason, Carl? It certainly isn't because you love me. Full sentence answers, please."

"I was afraid—scared about the results. I knew if the child was mine, our marriage would end. I do love you, Roxy. I wanted to feel you one more time."

"Pft! Nice try, Carl, but I don't buy the load of shit you're peddling. As usual, your dick was hard and your hand tired. You decided to stick it in the closest warm hole. Now, here's the bad news, at least for you: The question and answer session is over."

"You're going to kill me, aren't you?" Carl whispered.

Throwing my head back, I roared with laughter. "Carl Andrew! What kind of woman do you think I am? I'm the mother of your child, for Godsakes. Well, not the only mother, but the important one—I'm the first! Of course I'm not going to kill you. Oh, I thought about it, yet in the end, bearing your child saved your life. I won't put Carol through that kind of pain; which leads me to the next part of tonight's game. It's called: What Roxy Gets for Being Married to a Cheater. The Fifty Shades of Ginger round is over."

Carl's sigh of relief made his entire body vibrate. "Thank you."

A premature comment. My husband always had a problem with prematurity in the bedroom.

"Now, I'm going to unlatch one arm, you're going to flip over, grab the headboard, and hold still while I reattach the cuff. I wouldn't recommend trying anything foolish, because this knife is really sharp, and my temper is *really* short."

"Okay, whatever you want, Roxy. Whatever you want. Beat me into submission, I don't care. I deserve it."

Climbing off the bed, I unlatched one handcuff. Carl flipped over, his white ass up in the air, ready to take his punishment. To my surprise, he didn't offer up a fight. The second he was on his belly, his free hand grabbed the headboard. After re-attaching the cuff, I grimaced. "I never knew you were into bondage, Carl. Never. If I didn't know any better, I'd swear you're enjoying this."

"No, I'm not! I just want to make things right between us, Roxy. I deserve to be punished. Once you finish releasing your justified anger, maybe we can talk about this. I don't want our marriage to end."

"There's nothing left to say, darling," I purred. Backing up, I reached over and picked up the whip. It wasn't the kind you find at a sex shop. It was a real riding crop I bought at a tack store a few hours earlier. Knife in one hand, whip in the other, I climbed back onto the bed.

Carl was on all fours, shaking.

With a hard-on.

Whack!

"Oww! Jesus, Roxy! That hurt!"

"You lied. Rufus betrayed your true feelings about the situation. I told you not to lie to me!"

Whack!

Two bright, pink whelps appeared. Carl's erection disappeared after hitting him with all I had.

"I'm filing for divorce. Tomorrow. We're through."

Whack!

"Okay, okay!" Carl whimpered.

"I'm getting the house, alimony, you'll pay off my car, and I'll get half of your retirement and the money in savings. Credit card bills all land in your lap. Lucky for you Carol's got a free ride to college and is too old for child support, but you'll continue to pay her car payment, insurance, and help her out with expenses while in college."

Whack!

Oh, his ass is beet red, and I'm enjoying the hell out of this. Was I a closet dominatrix? No, I felt no sexual excitement, only rage.

"Okay! Okay! Whatever you want just please stop, Roxy!"

"Shut up!" *Whack!*

Carl's entire body shook with fear and pain.

"I won't tell a soul about your porn obsession or your impending fatherhood if I get all I want. You'll tell our daughter and others *after* the divorce is over about the baby. Try fucking with me, and you'll regret it. I copied the hard drive on your laptop and scanned your credit card statements today that show all your charges to online porn. Oh, and I downloaded all your texts and emails with not only Ginger, but others. Imagine my surprise when I realized you'd been humping Coco since she was *fourteen!* I told you she was jailbait. Now, all those things are in the hands of my attorney. I like to call them my aces in the hole. Just one little misstep, one item you try to cross me on, and I'll take it all to the president of the university. Guaranteed. Tenured or not, I doubt you'll retain your job when they find out you've been bumping uglies with a student and knocked her up."

Whack! Whack! Double Whack.

Carl sobbed uncontrollably as blood dripped off his torn-up rear onto the comforter. (Mental side note—stop by Bed Bath & Beyond tomorrow and purchase new sheets and comforter. This set is toast. Check!).

"We're both going to tell our daughter *you* decided to leave and the end of our marriage is *your* fault, not mine. You're having some sort of midlife crisis bullshit. Same goes for our friends. We simply grew apart and you decided to move out; which, by the way, will happen tonight. I've already packed your clothes and essential toiletries. They're in the study next to your destroyed laptop. I'm afraid I couldn't control myself after I realized Ginger wasn't your only sexual conquest. Pick all of it up when you leave. I'll tell Carol tonight when she comes home we're getting a divorce. I need to give her time to absorb the news before she starts school."

Whack! Whack!

"Please, stop! I'm so sorry, Roxy. I've got a problem, I know it. I couldn't help myself! It's not you, it's me. Those women meant nothing to me, I swear!"

"Pft! Women? You mean *girls.* Why don't you tell me something I don't already know? I've been the perfect wife! I serviced you, made sure to keep in shape so you'd be proud of your spouse—unlike you. I raised our daughter, maintained a spotless home, cooked every night, remained faithful to your little dick, and for what? For this ultimate betrayal? Do you have any idea how humiliated I was today, Carl? Opening the door and coming face-to-face with your whore? Your *pregnant* whore who thought I was your maid? I deserve way more than you've given me, Carl. Way more. I gave up my own hopes and dreams to be your better half and what do I get in return? Fucked over, that's what."

"Yes, you are a wonderful woman, Roxy. Again, it's me, not you. I didn't mean to hurt you. I swear!"

"Maybe, maybe not. However, I do mean to hurt you."

The final whack broke the handle of the riding crop. Carl screamed in agony.

Moving next to his face, I whispered: "Deviate one iota from my plans, Carl, and it will be the last thing you do. Oh, and if you have any aspirations of making *me* pay for tonight's fun, think again. I already informed my attorney that should anything happen to me, you know, like if you have the guts to try and kill me, or hire someone to do it, he's to release the documentation."

Carl's shoulders sagged as he cried.

"You'll never see me coming, or know what I've got up my sleeve, darling husband. Just like tonight's dinner. You ate dog food. And liked it."

Sobbing, Carl coughed twice then puked.

"You've got five minutes to get out of this house. Don't even think about stepping foot back inside. What's in here is all mine. Forever. The next time you see me will be in divorce court."

After I removed the cuffs, Carl collapsed forward, face landing in the hot vomit. He rolled away, wiping the chunks off his face. He stared at me, and for a second, I think he contemplated attacking me. I shook my head, brandishing the knife. The spark of anger in his eyes diminished, replaced by dejection and humiliation.

Without a word, Carl Andrew Davenport wrapped a towel around his waist, hobbled downstairs, gathered up his pre-packed belongings, and slithered out to the garage. In seconds, his precious, expensive toy roared to life.

Watching the taillights from the living room window, I stared in silence until they disappeared. Once gone, I glanced at my watch. Eight-fifteen. Oh, right on schedule. Damn, but I'm good!

Bounding up the stairs, in a rush to clean up the mess before Carol returned, I laughed. I needed to hurry so I'd have time to write down the night's fun in my journal so I could relive the memories for years to come.

While cleaning the mess upstairs, it dawned on me I was humming. God, I had crossed the line of sanity, done things I'd never thought I was capable of, all with a smile on my face and song on my lips.

Guess I'll always be a suburban housewife at heart, just one with a newly discovered mean streak.

A very, very mean streak.

That's certainly not in the *Handbook*, but it landed at the number six spot in my new one.

Roxy's New Rule Number Six: Release the inner beast when someone hurts you.

Check! I'd earned a bunch of credits tonight! No negative marks here, except on Carl's end. His *red*, bleeding rear end.

***

Twenty minutes before ten p.m., I finished removing all traces of the evening. Sweat dripped down my face while I bundled the trash bags up and carted them to the garage. It was time to celebrate with wine, smokes, and hot water, after adding my first adventure in the journal. My handwriting was atrocious as I scribbled on the pages.

Satisfied I'd entered enough to give me plenty of enjoyment

later, I hit the water. I needed to give my body and mind a treat before Carol arrived home. The wine would take the edge off my overtaxed brain before I told her the news.

Grabbing a full bottle of Moscato and the cigarettes, body clad in my demure one-piece, I entered the water. I managed to down two glasses and inhale three smokes when I heard Carol's VW Bug pull into the driveway.

"Sorry, baby. I know this is going to hurt, but believe me you'll thank me for it later. You'll figure out soon enough what kind of man your father is."

The front door slammed and Carol's footsteps drew closer. My heart pounded.

"Mom? Mom?"

Clearing my throat, I yelled: "In the hot tub, baby. Come join me! The water's perfect!"

My beautiful daughter appeared at the sliding glass doors, all young, fresh-faced, and full of innocence. I was angry at Carl before, but now, I downright hated him for the pain I was about to cause her.

"Put your suit on, honey. I want to hear all about your visit with Grandma."

Normally, Carol would scoff and ignore the offer. The last two years had pulled us apart. Maybe it was the look on my face, the cool breeze and inviting hot water, or simply that Carol wanted to spend time with me, knowing school would occupy all her time soon. Who knows? Whatever the reason, she nodded and disappeared back inside. Less than five minutes later, she joined me, dressed in strips of material sold as a bathing suit. Bra and panties cover more skin than the skimpy thing.

"So, how's Grandma?"

Carol's pert nose crinkled. "Same. She didn't recognize me or Liz. Well, not true. She still thinks I'm her friend Emma. It's so very sad. The vacant, distant look behind her eyes breaks my heart. Don't be mad, but I took one of the funeral card things—"

Stunned, I interrupted: "You took a remembrance announcement?"

"Yes. Please, don't be mad at me."

I softened my tone. "Honey, I'm not angry. Promise. I just wish you'd have waited until Aunt Becca or I were with you, in case Grandma had a moment of clarity and remembered. I wouldn't want you to deal with that on your own."

Carol blew out a huff of air. "Thanks for not being upset, Mom. It didn't matter, though. When I handed it to her, there was no spark of recognition. She stared at it for only a second then asked me if the girl who died was one from the old neighborhood. It's so sad. God, I don't think there's anything worse than losing your mind."

"I agree. A little piece of me dies every time I go see her. She looks so frail, so confused. Grandma's body is somewhat healthy for her age, but her mind isn't. When I'm old, I'd much rather my situation be the other way around."

Carol grimaced. "Don't talk like that, Mom. You're still young! All my male friends think you're a MILF."

"Gee, um, thanks for sharing?" I laughed.

"It's been a long day for me, so, may I?" Carol pointed at the bottle of Moscato. "I'm not going anywhere."

Following her gaze, I contemplated saying no. In the end, knowing it wouldn't be the first glass of wine she'd tasted, and certainly not the last given she was heading to college soon, and the news about her parents' divorcing was lingering, I acquiesced. "Just one."

"Three?" Carol countered.

"Two—and you'll need a glass."

Smiling, Carol stood and went to the outside bar and brought a wine glass back. After filling it to the rim, she slunk back into the tub. "How are you holding up, Mom? I know this has been really a rough last two weeks."

Choking back a lump of tears at how much Carol had changed

during the last few months, I contemplated saying something along those lines. I didn't, fearing if I dared broach the subject, even if said with flowery words and a huge grin, she might perceive the comment as a dig at her past behavior. It was wonderful to see and hear the concern in her voice, which I equated with love. "Don't worry about me, sweetheart. I'll be fine. I'm more concerned about how you're handling Aunt Rachel's death. I know how close you two were."

Carol's eyes filled with tears. "I miss her so much and can't believe I'll never get to talk to her again. I wanted her to see me graduate from college and veterinary school. You know, I had this mental plan of opening a vet clinic and asking her to work with me. It would be her dream job, and mine."

"That's so sweet. How come you never told me that before?"

Shrugging her shoulders, Carol took a long gulp of wine while staring at the water. "I don't know. Maybe I thought it was a silly, childish dream."

"Baby, it's not silly. It was a wonderful idea and Rachel would have loved it. You just stick to the original plan and follow your heart. It will be the best way to honor her memory."

"You really think so?"

"Of course I do. I've always urged you to follow your dreams, take the path that leads you to happiness and success." Well, that was a bald-faced lie—not to Carol but to myself—because I'd always hoped Carol would continue on the tradition of the Rayburn women since Rebecca didn't and Rachel couldn't. "I think your love of animals came from spending so much time with Rachel, so it seems a natural progression to become a vet."

"I guess," Carol answered while wiping a tear from her cheek. After clearing her throat, she asked: "Where's Dad? I didn't see his car in the garage. Is he out playing poker with the guys?"

Poker. The word had a whole new meaning to me now that I knew what *poker night* truly meant. Poke *Her*. Ha ha, very clever, men of the world. Very clever indeed. Though I was glad she'd changed the topic from Rachel, I dreaded the new direction of the conversation. Unfortunately, it couldn't be helped. "No, he's not."

"Then, where is he?"

Taking a deep breath, I downed the rest of my wine and immediately refilled it. "We need to talk about some things."

The back deck fell silent as my lovely daughter scanned my face. It didn't take long for her to read the signs. "He's not coming back, is he? You two are getting a divorce, right?"

I did one thing right in my life—I raised an astute young woman. "I'm afraid so, honey."

"He cheated on you, didn't he?" Carol hissed. "Can't say I'm surprised. Jesus! How many times did I defend him over the years when my girlfriends mentioned he was looking at them funny?"

I forced my mouth not to drop open from shock. Carol Claire Davenport didn't miss a thing, and apparently, neither did her friends.

"Oh, I'm sure they were mistaken, sweetheart. Your father didn't cheat on me! I know it sounds trite, but we've simply grown apart over the years and headed in different directions. Sometimes, the death of a loved one changes your perspective about things. Makes you question your life and such. What you've accomplished or what's missing from your life. Your dad hasn't been the same since his parents died."

"Bullshit, Mom. Gram and Grampa died four years ago. The only emotion he expressed was giddiness after buying his freaking car. I don't remember him shedding a tear at their funerals."

"Men from your father's generation were taught not to cry or show much outward emotion, sweetie. Don't hold that against him. He was devastated when they passed away. I believe it started the inner examination process. Rachel's death just added to it. He wants his freedom to explore new things in his life, so who am I to stop him from achieving what his heart desires?"

"His wife, that's who!" Carol yelled. "God, I'm so pissed right now! He leaves you the day after Aunt Rachel's funeral? What a jerk! I'm sorry, Mom. I really am. I know you love him, but he's a Grade-A asshole. Let him go. We'll get through this together, I promise."

"Yes, we will. Both of us are strong women."

"I'm strong, but you aren't."

Oh, I beg to differ. Your father's busted backside is proof!

"You've been Dad's doormat for years. Gave up your life to be a fucking housewife, and look what happened? I'm so glad you raised me to be independent, to not look to a man to make me feel complete. I think that's why you and I butted heads for so long."

Stunned, I replied: "What do you mean?"

"I mean," Carol responded then took another long swig of wine. "I would get angry at you, sometimes, because you are such a contradiction."

My mouth dropped open.

"Don't look like you're surprised, Mom. Come on! 'Don't take home economics, sweetie—I can teach you how to cook! Pick an elective you'll enjoy and that will actually help you out in life.' Remember that conversation, Mom? Or the ones every single time I talked about someone I was interested in you would say: 'Take your time, honey. You're too young to get serious.' You pushed me to be strong and independent, yet then would turn around and be subservient to Dad. It turned my stomach."

"Carol, honey, I've never been—"

"Don't try to deny it, Mom. I've watched you my entire life! Ugh! I had my doubts before about the whole traditional marriage lifestyle, but I don't anymore. It's not for me. Ever. There is no such thing as true love. It's nothing but an illusion concocted by jewelers, candy and card companies to make money."

Wow! When did my child turn into such a cynic? Had she been secretly spending time with L.B., the only other cynic I knew who could give me a run for the money? Rebecca Denise Rayburn did *not* marry for love. She married for prestige, comfort, and notoriety. Though her husband adored her, Rebecca's eyes and hands tended to wander when the good doctor wasn't around. "Carol, just because things didn't work out with our marriage, doesn't mean the same will happen to you! Just—do a better job than I did picking out the right man. Marry for the right reasons, unlike us. We tried to make it work, but it simply didn't. End of story."

"I don't need a man, anyway. I can achieve the same satisfaction with a vibrator and then stuff it into a drawer when finished. Easy-peasy, and no fear of unwanted pregnancies or STDs."

"Carol!" I laughed so hard I choked on my wine.

Leaning over to hug me, Carol smiled. "Sorry, couldn't help myself. I wanted to make you laugh, and it worked. Don't worry, Mom. I'll help you get through this. So will Liz, Aunt Becca, and all your other friends. Between us all, you'll be just fine. That's a promise. Now, I'll finally be like all my other friends, instead of the odd one of the bunch."

"What do you mean?"

"Mom, all of my friends, every one of them, came from broken homes. I was the weirdo with parents still married. Now, I won't be."

The tears I'd held inside since Hottie Habanero appeared and dropped the bomb in my lap, broke free. Sobbing in my daughter's arms, I wept for what I thought I had, what I really had, and what would never be. The tears of sadness were mixed with ones of pride I felt for my daughter. My sweet little girl was the freaking Rock of Gibraltar!

A few drips were from the concerns over the vicious person I'd become. Honestly, she scared the hell out of me.

Demerit. Demerit. Too many fucking demerits to count.

CHAPTER 5

Book Club Revelations

I dreaded book club. This wasn't a first, but today, I *really* dreaded it. Other than L.B., Carl, Carol, and my attorney, I hadn't told a soul about the divorce. However, that would all change when everyone got around to reading the newspaper. Reginald filed today, which meant the case of *Roxanne D. Davenport vs. Carl Andrew Davenport* would be listed in the legal section, and the topic of discussion tonight rather than the stupid erotic romance.

Ugh.

True to my sister's narcissistic ways, she'd yet to stop by, call or text me (Rebecca's preferred way of contact, just like her personality: Cold and boring) and enquire as to why my marriage was kaput. It didn't affect Rebecca's life one bit, so why would she strain her arm to pick up the phone and call? Risk ruining an expensive manicure by texting? Waste her precious fucking time by dropping by after work?

She wouldn't, not unless the effort benefited the uptight wife of Dr. Wilson in some way. Though she lived a block away, we rarely spoke. The week Rachel fell ill and died had been the first time we'd talked so much since, oh, pretty much ever. She even left me high and dry when our mother's health went south.

As usual, since I was the oldest, I'd been responsible for handling Mom's mental issues and living arrangements. Rebecca had nothing to do with the entire process and let me be the one to sign the dotted line putting Mom into a memory care facility. Rachel wasn't helpful, either. My flighty baby sister was a basket case once the diagnosis of dementia left the lips of Mom's doctor. All Rachel could do was cry.

Jesus, I hate being the oldest. And I miss my baby sister like crazy. What I wouldn't give to hear her voice just one more time. If still alive, Rachel would be right by my side, offering support and a loving hug. She'd be full of inspirational words, assuring me things would be fine, and we'd get through the bump in the road together.

Dammit!

The relationship with Rebecca was screwed-up, yet when something happened to Rachel, from stubbing her toe to breaking up with yet another loser, Rebecca and I closed ranks. We surrounded our communal baby sister with an impenetrable wall of protective estrogen. Once the crisis was over, we disbanded quicker than liquid dish soap and oil. Yes, we traveled in the same social circles, attending monthly book club meetings together, etc., but all of our interactions in public were just great acting jobs on both our parts. We only made it through the holidays because of booze.

So, it wasn't surprising Rebecca didn't offer up any sort of encouragement or support. Hell, she'd probably been celebrating at home each night, dancing around the living room, spilling wine, laughing, at my expense.

At my pain.

Bitch.

Staring at the most recent demented ramblings in my journal, I sighed. The last week was sort of a blur, spent drinking too much wine and passing out in bed, after pretending things were normal until Carol went to sleep. Though I'd never admit it to anyone, I felt sort of lost and hollow. The emptiness wasn't from missing Carl. Our marriage had been over for years, though keeping up the façade we were a happy couple obviously took up a lot of my energy.

Sleeping alone in the California King-sized bed was nice. No nocturnal emissions from Carl's nasty ass; no fumbling hands reaching for me underneath the sheets. I could flop around, toss and turn all I wished, without rousing my grumbling spouse.

I hadn't heard a peep from ol' Carl since the night he scurried away like a whipped dog. Not one phone call, text, or email. Zip. Zilch. Nada. I could only assume he'd shown up on Hottie Habanero's doorstep, ass bleeding and pride wounded, begging the little knocked-up tamale to take him in. Did she? If so, the little tramp surely got an earful about her lover's interesting evening with his soon-to-be-ex! Guess my little spanking session worked as I intended. Score one for me!

Prior to this nightmare, a part of me had been proud to be one of the last of a dying breed—a woman who stayed at home, took care of things from A–Z, carried on the tradition passed down from previous generations. I'd been the one others ran to for advice when problems in their homes arose, just like my mother had been with her friends. With a divorce looming above my head, I wouldn't be the "Go-To Woman" anymore.

The sad truth was now I was just another statistic. A single woman over forty, her exhusband hooked up with a younger slut, leaving the bewildered ex-wife to pick up the pieces of her broken life.

I simply didn't know what to do with myself on a daily basis. Carol left and headed to work each day, and spent a lot of time at night with her girlfriends. There was no family meal to plan out, no reason to keep the house spotless. Everything was turned upside down, and I shouldered part of the blame.

I wanted things to change; convinced myself to shift directions, move away from the old ways and create new ones.

"Oh, stop it, Roxy! No more whining! You can do this!"

Roxy's New Rule Number Seven: Kill off the old woman so the new one can take over.

Satisfied with the latest rule, I flipped back a few pages and read the previous week's entries, Yikes! They were full of dark, ugly thoughts and gore-filled details about how I'd kill Ginger, Coco, and Carl, along with countless other whores my husband screwed.

Seems my drunken mind nailed Roxy's New Rules Six and Seven! Check!

I need to stop drinking because, apparently, too much booze turns me into a sadistic killer. Wait, give up my Moscato? What am I thinking? No way! Besides, I was sober when I whipped Carl's ass. Alcohol had nothing to do with releasing my inner monster, so why punish myself by depriving my screwed-up brain of wine?

I'd yet to tell Liz, even when she called the day after Carl's punishment, expecting a load of details about the experiment in the bedroom. I sidestepped the conversation, telling her I had numerous things to accomplish, including taking over ownership of Mom's house, sending out thank you cards to those who'd attended Rachel's service, etc. Liz prodded, but backed off after I promised to spill the details over coffee a few hours before book club.

The truth was I had been busy the previous week. I had spent one entire day going through all of Rachel's belongings in her apartment which, thankfully, didn't take too long. Rachel didn't have much since she bounced from one job to the next. I packed up all her clothes and took them to Goodwill, called a donation company to come pick up the minimal furniture, and brought one box home full of memorabilia from our childhood, and a few pictures.

God, that day sucked, and ended with too many bottles of wine.

Plus, I changed cell providers for my phone and Carol's; opened a new bank account in only my name; called all the utilities and removed Carl's name. I stood by and watched a fat, crack-showing representative install new locks on the doors. My days were filled with lots of new tasks, and my frazzled mind soothed at night with copious amounts of wine. At the current pace I was drinking, I needed to go work at a liquor store just for the discount.

Looking at my watch, I grimaced. Liz would knock on the door any second and I wasn't sure I could pull off lying to her face and getting away with it. Liz knew all my facial expressions better than her own. She'd sniff out a fib in seconds.

If she noticed anything amiss, I'd simply blame my sour demeanor on my visit with Mom. That part wasn't a lie, for every time I went to see her, I'd mope around for at least twenty-four hours, heartbroken and reliving the days when Mom's mind was still sharp.

***

My thoughts wandered to the earlier visit with Mom. Inside her smelly room, my body crammed into an uncomfortable chair on the other side of the plastic table, I'd told my mother the news of my impending divorce. Of course, since she had no clue who the hell I was, the sordid tale didn't faze her in the least. Since she wouldn't remember the visit, or the words spoken for more than three minutes, I spilled my dark secrets and told her everything.

Every. Single. Detail.

Her response when I finished baring my soul? "That's quite a story, ma'am. Sounds like the poor woman deserved every bit of her revenge. Hope she gets all she wants out of life now that the awful husband is out of the picture. You know, men are like that.

They use us up, taking, until we're unable to give another drop, and then toss us aside like a dirty towel. You should take my advice and do like I did: Never get married, uh, oh, I'm sorry. What was your name again, sweetie?"

I'd choked back tears when she patted my hand, her eyes revealing not one hint of recognition of who I was, or the fact she'd been married to my amazing father. Knowing she'd dismissed me from her mind was one thing—knowing the memory of my beloved father had been completely wiped away from her mind made my chest heavy with sadness. I'd given her a fake name, one I can't quite recall, hugged her neck and then fled the facility as though someone was chasing me with an ax.

***

The doorbell rang and I jumped, spilling water all over my dress. Dandy. Oh well, at least the distraction kept me from thinking about Mom. Snatching up the journal, I headed to the kitchen to grab a dish towel and hide my murderous ramblings in the drawer. "Come on in, Liz. The door's open."

Liz walked down the hallway and into the dining room while I wiped up the water. From the corner of my eye, I noticed she took in the visual of my messy house.

Demerit!

"Hey, sweetie. You should have told me you've been sick. I don't mind helping out around here. Can't count how many times you've done the same for me over the years. God knows we can't rely on our husbands or children to lift a finger. Did you catch the flu or something?"

Joining her at the table, I forced a smile. "Do I look that bad?"

Studying every inch of my face, noting the disheveled hair and lack of makeup, Liz grimaced. "Don't hate me for saying so, but yes. Have you been to the doctor?"

"Yes. He gave me a clean bill of health. I'm not sick, just tired."

Again, another tidbit of truth, mixed with a lie. I did go to see Dr. Critchon, but only to have him draw blood and test me for every possible STD on the planet. I counted the negative results as a miracle, considering Carl's fifteen years of sticking his dick into strange pussy.

Bastard! I should have gone ahead and castrated him and kept the small piece of flesh as a trophy. It would have been fun to wear the shriveled piece of skin as a reminder of how I took care of business!

"Of course you are, given the last few weeks. Sorry. It was rude of me to assume you're sick, rather than in mourning. Did you go see Claire today, too? I know visiting with her knocks the wind out of you."

"Yes, and it certainly does. I really miss talking to her and knowing she'll answer me back as my mom, not a stranger."

Liz didn't respond, she simply stared at me with her huge brown eyes. Yes, she could read my emotions, and I had the same ability to recognize hers.

She knew, and my best friend waited with the patience of a saint for me to come clean.

Sighing, I stood and went to the liquor cabinet. After setting two glasses and a bottle of wine in between us, I whispered: "You know, don't you?"

A few tears glistened in Liz's eyes as she nodded.

Pouring us both a glass, I sat, unwilling to meet her gaze. "I'm sorry I didn't tell you before, I just couldn't. Needed to wrap my head around it first and help Carol deal with the news before telling others."

"Oh, honey! Please don't apologize. God, I'm so sorry, and frankly, stunned. Out of all the couples I know, you two seemed so, I don't know, made for each other?"

"People grow apart. Hit enough speed bumps in life and eventually the car falls apart."

"Glad your sense of humor is still on target. Jesus, Roxy. What are you going to do? Is Carl trying to get the house? Weasel out of alimony?"

"What I'm going to do is let him go. He wanted a new life, he can have it. In terms of our assets, Carl's being quite liberal with things. Since it was his choice to leave, he decided to take what he could carry in his car and call things even."

Liz's eyebrows popped up in shock. "Are you serious? What did you do? Drug him and make him sign something? I don't recall you two having a prenup!"

I almost told her the truth, eager to see the look of shock on her face, but I wasn't ready to let others see the new, darker side. "No, nothing like that. He wants a clean slate to start a new life with, and to keep things amicable between us. You know, for Carol's sake? Though sad, the process has been rather easy."

Thanks to a sharp knife, my stellar planning skills, and a riding crop. *Whack! Whack! Whack!*

"How's Carol taking the news?"

"That girl is tougher than aged leather. She almost sounded, I don't know, relieved? Mentioned she'd no longer be the weirdo with parents married to their original spouses. I found that rather sad. Suburbia is changing so fast."

"No doubt. Us old dinosaurs are a dying breed," Liz sighed, taking a long drink of wine. "So, I assume the reasons you had me occupy Carol's time last Friday were false?"

Okay, pull off the lie, Roxy. Sell it like you sold fake orgasms for years. "No, I had every intention of doing what I told you over the phone. Something in the back of my mind urged me to spice things up, sensing trouble brewing. Instead of an erotic, romance-filled evening like expected, our marriage broke in two."

"No wonder you didn't want to talk about it and brushed me off! What an asshole! He dumps you the very next day after Rachel's funeral? Argh! I could strangle him for being such an insensitive prick!"

Join the club, sister. Join the club.

The urge to tell Liz the truth was driving me crazy. I decided to throw her a bone, thereby releasing some of the pressure from my mind. "I did get a bit of payback."

A devious grin spread across Liz's full lips. "Do tell! Hope you slapped the fire out of him. No, better yet! Kicked him in the crotch! Oh, who am I kidding? That's not your personality at all. You talk a good game sometimes yet you don't even step on spiders!"

Way more than that, dear friend. Way more. *Whack! Whack!*

"No, nothing like that. I was, uh, in the middle of cooking dinner, all dressed in a sexy outfit, ready to spice things up when he dropped the bomb. I started crying, and he went to pour himself a drink. So, while I had the chance, I altered the meatloaf."

"With what? Rat poison?" Liz laughed.

"Dog food. Beef Medley, to be exact. Carl ate two platefuls!"

Both of us burst into loud cackles. God, it was so nice to enjoy a good belly laugh.

"That's hysterical! I can't believe you did that, though part of me wishes you'd kicked him in the nuts, too."

Liz's phone and mine buzzed several times. Someone was hitting us up. We exchanged knowing glances, fully aware the freak circus of my life was the subject matter.

"Sasha and Denise just heard," Liz muttered.

"Yep, they both sent texts to me, too."

My phone rang and I winced at the number. "Excuse me for a second, Liz. I've got to take this call."

In a rush, I opened the sliding glass doors and stepped out onto the back deck. Walking far enough away that I knew Liz wouldn't be able to hear me, I answered the call from Dr. Critchon's office. "Hello?"

"Mrs. Davenport?"

"Yes," I responded as a shroud of worry settled over my chest. If he was about to tell me they read a test wrong and I did have some sort of STD, I feared what my response might be.

"I'd like to schedule an appointment with you during the next week. We need to discuss some—"

"Is this your PC way of trying to tell me my vagina is going to rot away soon?" I interrupted.

"No, Mrs. Davenport. As I told you before, you are free and clear of any sexually transmitted diseases."

"Then why in the world do I need to come see you? Is it my heart? High blood pressure? Diabetes? Worse? I'm pregnant?"

Now *that* would be the real icing on the cake! Perhaps my ovaries woke up unexpectedly.

"It's not something we should discuss over the phone."

My heart skipped three beats and I felt dizzy. There was no way I could wait days to find out exactly what the cryptic words meant. "I've got a lot going on, as you know, so tell me now. What's wrong with me?"

In stunned silence, I listened to Dr. Critchon prattle on about what the blood tests revealed about my health. After all I've been through, I certainly didn't think things could get worse yet they just did. My mouth went dry and my entire body started to shake.

"Mrs. Davenport? Are you still there?"

"Uh, yes. Sorry. Just trying to digest the news."

"I still would like for you to come to the office so we can discuss the ramifications and treatment options in person before the disease progresses. I have an opening on Monday at three."

"See you then," I responded then disconnected the call.

This. Isn't. Happening.

Numbed from shock, I stared at the pool, trying to pull myself together before going back inside. Too bad the human brain can't react the same as a computer to Cntl-Alt-Del. Damnit! Why now? The cosmos just rained a pile of shit balloons over my head and they all popped at the same time.

I heard the sliding glass doors open and Liz step out, followed by the flick of a lighter. *Suck it up, Roxy. Think about the news later.*

"You look like you need one," Liz whispered while handing me a cigarette. "Was that your lawyer with bad news like Carl's changed his mind and wants a dirty fight?"

Taking the smoke, I inhaled long and deep. "Something like that, yes. God, I don't think I can handle book club tonight, Liz. Facing them will be too much."

"Bullshit. You have nothing to be ashamed of, Roxy. I won't let you cower inside this house like a whipped dog. Come on—you get in the shower while I rummage around your closet for the sexiest outfit you own. Then, I'll help you with hair and makeup, and you're going to strut your hot body into Sasha's house, a smile on your face, and prove to those grousing harpies you aren't wallowing in a pit of sorrow. Then, after it's over, we can sit down and figure out the best plan of action for the divorce. Okay?"

"I don't know, Liz."

Grabbing my hand, Liz forced me to stand. "I do. Trust me on this. You'll lean on me until strong enough to stand alone. I've got your back. Promise."

God, what would I do without my Liz?

I'd keep the old Rule Number Seventeen about a best friend.

No doubt.

Touching my head, I grimaced. There was so much product in my hair it felt like the Eighties all over again. The days of carrying big purses stuffed with—at a minimum—two cans of Aqua Net and mousse. Bam, I just stepped back in time. The only thing missing to recreate the times Liz and I did each other's hair and makeup was a stereo blaring "Controversy," by Prince (my favorite song—ever!) in the background.

My God, I wore every one of his albums out. The man was a musical genius, though, during my younger years, I gravitated to his music for the beat. As I aged, it was all about the deep meaning behind the words. Liz was more of a headbanger. We did alternate musical choices sometimes, though only if we were at her house getting ready. Liz loved "Looks that Kill," by Motley Crue. Her father, the oh-so-serious brain surgeon, Dr. Gelmini, was another story. He'd yell "turn that racket off!" from downstairs.

Staring at my reflection in the bathroom mirror, I couldn't help but laugh. "It looks fantastic, Liz. Truly. But, when I get home later, it's going to take an entire bottle of shampoo to get all this out. I appreciate you not caking six layers of makeup on me, though. I like this minimal look. Very dramatic, plus it makes me look younger. What's this lipstick color again?"

"Video Vixen."

"Ha! Guess it's true—styles from the past always resurface. Thank God, the jelly shoe trend hasn't re-emerged. I hated those uncomfortable things!"

"Me, too. I've got scars on the back of my heels from blisters. Between us, I think we owned at least twenty pairs! Now, stand up and let me take a good look at you."

"Fine," I muttered, blushing. I never liked to be ogled, which was another reason I worked out at home. My boobs bouncing around tended to make men run into things.

"Holy shit, you're smoking hot! God, if my tits looked half as good, Roger would never let me leave the bedroom. If I was a carpet muncher, I'd take you home with me and lick you dry."

"Uh, thanks? Wow, that came out of nowhere. I thought I was the comedienne out of our duo. Don't confuse me. I'm the funny one and you're the serious one."

"Come on, it's time to go show off the masterpiece that is Roxy Davenport! Turn those plastic faces green with envy. Here," Liz said, holding out a pair of black stilettos. "Put them on. You're quite the imposing sight at nearly 6' 1" in these babies."

"I can't walk all the way to Sasha's in these things! I'll fall and bust my ass."

Liz rolled her eyes. "No, you'll roll those hips and sway that ass. A few catcalls and beeping horns will boost your self-esteem. Hurry."

Sliding the painful shoes on, I followed Liz downstairs. Carol looked up from the book she was reading in the living room, giving a low whistle. "Whoa, sexy Mama!"

Blushing, I laughed. "We're heading to book club, sweetie. Be back in a few hours. Dinner's in the fridge. I want to hear all about school when I get back. Love you."

"Love you, too, Mom. Show those uptight bitches what's what."

"That's the plan, girl. Between the two of us, we'll keep your mom afloat."

Smiling at Liz and Carol, appreciative of their support, I strutted with purpose out the front door, Liz right beside me.

"Give me your arm before I fall," I whispered.

"You won't. Just keep your head high, shoulders back, and gaze straight ahead. Own it. Work it. Pretend you're Sasha, just higher-class."

We strolled down the sidewalk toward Sasha's, smiling and laughing as whistles and shouts from our neighbors greeted us.

"Oh, Roxy! You look great! That's the way to do it—show that bastard what he's missing!"

Sasha gave me a light hug, blowing air-kisses in my ear. Her stinky, cheap perfume made my eyes water. Sasha was married to a former pro athlete and lived on the *good* side of town now, but all the money, clothes, makeup, fancy car, and house still didn't hide who she'd been prior to marrying up.

You can move the whore uptown, but she's still a whore at heart. Sasha was living proof.

Denise piped up from behind me. "Carl's a fool, Roxy. A damn fool. His loss, not yours. With that body and face, you'll snag another man in no time! Wow, you're such an inspiration. Lost your sister and husband in the space of one week, and look better than all of us put together. Bitch!"

Sasha ushered us inside to the living room, pausing once to hand us both drinks. Liz beamed as we took our usual seats on the plush couch.

For the next fifteen minutes, as Sasha's home filled with book club members, the topic of conversation was me. The room of women I'd dreaded seeing surprised me with their support and gushing words, even though most of it was sprinkled with underlying jealousy about the way I looked. Sasha even asked at one point if I'd had a chemical peel because, she said, I was radiant.

Pft. I'm glowing because I finally let the real me out of her mental cage. Whoopie!

I stuck to the contrived story about growing apart, midlife crisis crap, and the ladies bought into it. Carl's name was dragged through the mud, which was rather fun, and lessened the sting of the barbed comments.

The fun ended when Denise asked: "Where's Elaine?"

"Well, I swore I wouldn't tell," Sasha gushed.

The three glasses of wine she'd downed while rambling on about what a piece of shit Carl Davenport was, and most men in general, loosened her tongue. This wasn't something new, for Sasha Rice didn't need alcohol to help her spread gossip. Liz and I secretly nicknamed her Sling-It Sasha.

The woman had a lot of nerve spilling gossip. Jesus, the stories she'd shared with me about her bedroom activities with Jermaine, and others, made the erotic romance novel we were supposed to be discussing look tame. Sasha would go from dark, chocolate skin to white cocoa if I opened my mouth and shared her dirty laundry. So would Denise and the others. For some reason, the women seemed to forget they had a habit of coming to me in private, sharing their disgusting exploits. Denise and her husband enjoyed role play, and had even swapped spouses a few times with Sasha and Jermaine. Neither one of the bags had a clue the other had told me, and I kept my word and never told a soul. Not even Liz.

Idiots.

"But you're going to anyway since you can't keep a secret from your besties, right?" Denise urged, her blue eyes dancing with eager anticipation.

"Or her legs together when the pool boy is around!" Jeanette Dickson added, giggling.

"I may give the boy a show now and then, but he's never cleaned this undercarriage!" Sasha laughed.

"Sasha, stay on topic! Why isn't Elaine here? She never misses book club, and I know she's been dying to talk about the erotic novel! Is she sick or something?" Denise groused.

Lowering her voice, Sasha shook her head. "She isn't sick, but Coco is, er, was."

"What does that mean, Sasha?" Jeanette prodded.

"It means," Sasha rubbed her flat stomach, "that the sickness was removed yesterday, sparing Coco and Elaine a lifetime of embarrassment."

My stomach dropped.

Denise gasped. "Are you saying Coco was—?"

"Yep," Sasha cut off Denise's words. "Knocked up at sixteen. Elaine made her get an abortion yesterday. She's beyond devastated her future model was deflowered."

My vision blurred and a weird buzzing sound filled my head. I caught only snippets of the remainder of the hen party as my mind burned with fury, shame, and humiliation. No, it couldn't be Carl's! Though I despised Blow-Up Barbie, she was a knockout. There was no way Coco's slit only welcomed Carl's dick. She had to be giving it up to other, younger men—hot studs with bulging biceps and erections lasting for more than ten minutes that arose naturally rather than from little blue pills.

Okay, stop freaking out. If the little bun in Coco's oven was placed there, courtesy of random Rufus sperm, the evidence was all gone. It seemed Coco was keeping her mouth shut, which was probably a first. I wonder how many times she'd sucked on ol' Raging Rufus? Did she nickname Carl's cock, too? Knowing her ditzy ass, it was something even more ridiculous than Rufus, like Krull or The Thing.

Gag. Triple gag. Dammit! Had Carl fucked every female in

Cherrywood Estates? Damn him and those puppy-dog eyes and sensual smile. He wasn't supposed to use them on anyone but me!

My ears perked up when Denise said: "I'm surprised Mr. Shock hasn't been arrested. He's certainly the type to take out his anger physically. Remember what he did to the car of the man who rear-ended him last year? And the man? He beat them both up! Maybe he doesn't know? Did Elaine and Coco keep it a secret from him?"

"Oh, he knows. Coco just refuses to give up the identity of the father. She's knows how her daddy is about his precious daughter. According to Elaine, he took his anger out on the hedges in the backyard and cut them all down to the ground! Bet he was imagining cutting something else with the clippers!"

"Ladies, enough!" Liz interjected. "We're supposed to be shredding apart the latest book, not each other!"

"Look who's on her high horse," Rebecca slurred from the hallway.

Oh, this night just keeps getting better and better! I wanted to kick myself for letting Liz convince me to come. I should be home, drunk, lamenting the twists and turns of my life, and plotting out the gruesome deaths of my enemies, like Coco and Ginger.

"Just arrived and already sauced?" Denise shot back.

Plopping down on a chair, Rebecca smiled. It was anything but nice or friendly. "It's been a really long day. Forgive me for indulging before I arrived. What did I miss? Who should be getting beat up?"

It took everything in me to remain seated. I wanted to leave, but I didn't. I knew the minute I left Sasha's living room my troubles would be open season once they finished ripping the Shock family to pieces. I'd make the uncaring, cold-hearted bitches wait to shred my life apart.

So, as per my usual experience at book club, I remained quiet and listened, only offering a few "Uh-huhs" or "I agree" and even the occasional "That's awful" to the discussion. An hour later, mind wandering to places it didn't need to visit, Rebecca's drunk ass tottered over, swaying in front of me.

"Excuse us for a moment. Smoke break."

"Make sure to take something to put the spent butts in," Sasha urged. "Jermaine was pissed after our last meeting."

"Of course, Sasha," Rebecca cooed.

I knew that tone. It meant Sasha's back deck would be littered with dead smokes before we left. Wouldn't surprise me if Rebecca ran to her car, retrieved the ashtray, and dumped the contents all over.

Once out back, Rebecca lit up and so did I.

"Thanks. I needed this. Listening to them grouse was making me—"

"I didn't save you from those witches for nothing, Roxy. We need to talk. Well, I'll talk and you'll listen."

This can't be good. If she was about to tell me she'd fucked Carl, too, I'd lose my mind. "About?"

"You and your situation, idiot. What else?"

God, sisterhood. Gotta love it! "You're concerned now? Gee, it only took you a week. You must be growing a heart, Grinch."

Glowering at me, Rebecca snorted. "It took me a week to go over things, figure out the best course of action. Excuse me for trying to keep you out of the poor house."

"Come again?"

"You forget, big sis, I'm your accountant. I know how much is in the bank, what you owe on the house, cars, and credit cards. What's in Carl's retirement account and the amount left from his inheritance."

I didn't like where this was going. At all. "What are you getting at, L.B.?"

"I'm saying you're going to be in a hurt locker without a job."

"I'll be fine. Carl's already agreed to my terms. I get the house, my car paid off, credit cards out of my name, alimony, half of his retirement—"

Rebecca put a finger to my lips, shushing me. I contemplated butting her head with my own.

"Roxy, shut up and listen! You can get all of that, and it still won't matter. Have you forgotten how much the yearly real estate taxes are on that enormous monstrosity you live in? How much the attorney fees will be for this divorce? The possibility the judge may not let you have all you want? What then? What if something happens to Carl?"

"Well, uh," I stuttered.

"Yeah, that's what I thought. You have no idea. It's a good thing I'm the levelheaded one. I've solved your dilemma, which is why I haven't contacted you all week. I've been trying to figure out the best solution to this issue, and I finally did."

Curious, yet still wary, I asked: "And the solution would be?"

"You need a job. Not some piss-ant minimum wage job. To stay in the house, continue to live close to the same lifestyle, you need a good paying position. Forty grand per year plus benefits will give you the ability to breathe and not stress about money."

Snorting, I laughed. "Gee, I hadn't thought about that! Oh, wait, yes, I did. I nixed the idea because those types of jobs simply aren't available for someone with my limited work skills. Period."

"Yes, I'm aware. That's why I already found you a job."

My jaw dropped. "If you're about to suggest I work a pole or a street corner like Sasha, I'm going to beat your ass."

"You're too old for that type of work, dear sister. I believe 25 is the cutoff," Rebecca snapped back. "As I said, I found a *workable* solution not a fantasy."

Fuck you, L.B. "You did? Seriously? No bullshit?"

"Cross my heart, sis. No bullshit."

A spark of excitement made my heart pound. "Doing what? Where?"

The teasing look on Rebecca's face changed. Now, she looked

like a spider ready to pounce on the fly trapped in the sticky web. "Accounting. I need an assistant because mine just put in her two weeks' notice."

It took several seconds for the foreign words to sink in. When they did, I laughed so hard my sides hurt and I worried I might lose control of my bladder. "You? Work for you? Are you high? Reliving the Eighties by doing blow again?"

"Not funny, Roxy," Rebecca whined, a slender finger reaching up involuntarily to touch the tip of her nose.

"We can't handle being in a room together for more than an hour without going for the jugulars, and you want to spend forty hours each week together? As my boss? Um, no thanks. I'd rather flip burgers or gouge my eyes out with hot pokers. Be drawn and quartered; burned at the stake. Suffer a massive stroke and keel over in the driveway."

"That's mean, Roxy. I'm your sister! When Mom's gone, we'll be all the family each other has left. I need an assistant and you need a job. You're going through a really tough time because your husband is a slimy douchebag, and I have the ability to make things easier for you. End of story. You start Monday at 8 a.m. Don't be late."

Before I could get any words to pop out of my gaping mouth, Rebecca was gone. I stood there looking like a fish struggling for air, mind stunned by the offer. The job would give me a legitimate excuse to cancel the appointment with Dr. Rotten-News. Not that I needed one—I didn't plan on going anyway—but in case he groused when I called to cancel the appointment, I wouldn't look like a terrified fool. The part of my brain in charge of handling the Davenport finances knew Rebecca was right; agreed her solution was a viable offer.

The other part, the older sister who despised the younger lunatic, hated the idea. Rebecca had gone through assistants like tampons: Use them up then toss them in the trash. I had no desire to be treated like a bloody feminine product.

***

"Roxy? You okay?"

Blinking twice, I glanced over at Liz, who stood in the doorway. "Uh, yeah. Just finishing this smoke."

Liz stepped out and shut the sliding glass door. "You mean the one that isn't lit yet?"

"Yeah, that one."

"What's going on? Were you and Rebecca arguing? You look upset."

Shaking my head, I let out a low chuckle. "Arguing? No, but I sort of wish we were, because I think I might have just suffered a stroke or someone spiked my wine and I'm hallucinating."

"Not funny, Roxy. What happened?"

Lighting the smoke, I took a deep drag. "Well, it seems L.B. is using the opportunity of being without an assistant, again, to her advantage. She wants me to work for her."

Liz blinked several times. "I'm sorry, but I think your stroke is contagious. Did you just say Rebecca wants you to work for *her*? And she was serious—not joking?"

"Dead serious. She expects me to be at work on Monday."

"Give me that," Liz chirped, snatching the smoke from my fingers.

"No! You quit!"

"Yes, I did, but I sneak them now and again when shocked or upset. You just shocked the hell outta me, so share."

"Fine," I muttered, letting her take the cigarette. I pulled another from my purse and lit up. "I don't know what I'm going to do. If she's serious and this isn't some sadistic prank, it's a good deal. Great money. Benefits. Work experience. I mean, hell, if I can suck it up and work for that lunatic bitch for a year or so, I'll be able to get a job anywhere."

Liz laughed. "That's true! Her reputation in the business world is legendary. Does this mean you're actually considering doing it?"

"Why the hell not? Everything else in my life is up in the air, so maybe a job will help ground me. Things can't get any worse, right? Besides, I lived with her for years. If she pisses me off or tries to get all bossy, I know which buttons to push to send her into the stratosphere. Did it all the time when we were little."

"I need another drink. No, several."

Stubbing out the smoke, I laughed. "Why? I'm the one going to work for the Queen Bitch, not you."

"Because, once book club is over, I'm going home and fucking Roger's brains out. I don't want to lose him and be forced to go work for my sister. I'd kill Tanya. Guaranteed."

***

Laughing, we returned to the living room, just as the long-awaited discussion of the book was underway. For the next half-hour, the fake hags laughed and giggled, actually blushing for Godsakes, when certain chapters were the topic of conversation, especially Chapter 37.

That's it. I'd heard enough. Let them talk about me and the demise of my marriage when I walked out the door, I didn't care.

"I'm going to call it a night, ladies. It's been a really long week, and I need to go check on Carol. She had freshman orientation today, and I'm dying to know how it went. Enjoy the rest of the discussion. Oh, and next month, can we please pick something other than a romance or smut? I'm ready for a thriller."

Rising to her feet, Sasha put her hand on my elbow, giving me a fake smile. Her dental implants were so white they could double as a flashlight in a pinch. "Of course, we understand. Go, take care of Carol. She's such a wonderful girl, and I'm sure the news has devastated her. Sheesh! Right before school starts. Carl's such a bastard. I'll walk you out."

Liz rose, too, but I motioned for her to stay. "I'll call you tomorrow, Liz. Ladies, have a nice night."

***

Sasha led me to the front door. "Goodness, what's the neighborhood coming to? First you and Carl are kaput and then this whole sordid mess with Coco? It's so sad. I always thought living in suburbia was a buffer from the sins of the city."

Something about her tone, the underlying superiority, infuriated me. Yanking my arm away, I leaned closer and whispered: "You're such a hypocrite, Sasha! You've got a lot of nerve spouting off your little act of shock and innocence. The others may buy it, but I know the *real* you, and exactly what street corner you worked, along with how you got pregnant with Jermaine's baby on purpose. Remember telling me? Adding in how you like to get all nasty and funky in the bedroom because part of you misses the old days? No, you probably don't. You were so drunk when you spilled your secrets you couldn't even walk."

Sasha's jaw dropped open.

"Not only did you tell me all the disgusting details, but the ones you left out, Denise filled me in on. That hoochie of yours has been around the block more times than Mrs. Goldberg walking her dog during the last ten years. Actually, I'm surprised it still works after all the abuse it's taken. From now on, maybe you should think before unleashing gossip, because one day, you might be on the receiving end, and I don't think you'd like it."

Sasha's big brown eyes widened. "Roxy! What's gotten into you? Why would you say such—?"

"I'm sick and tired of your pious attitude, Sasha, and your fake friendship. That's what's gotten into me. Elaine Shock thinks you're her best friend! She entrusted you with painful, sensitive events in her life and what did you do? Opened that big mouth of yours and spilled the beans. Imagine her surprise had she overheard you earlier! Would you have said the same things, or even brought the subject up, if Elaine had been here? That's a rhetorical question, so don't bother answering. You wouldn't.

You'd pour out a bunch of fake concern, cooing and grousing, trying to be supportive if Elaine *opted* to tell the rest of us. Grow up, bitch. This isn't high school or one of those staged reality shows you love to watch. This is real life, with real feelings and families on the line. Act like an adult for once and show a little class."

Leaving a stunned Sasha on the stoop, I turned and left, satisfied with myself for finally saying things I'd wanted to for years.

Roxy's New Rule Number Eight: Put obnoxious, fake friends in their place.

Check!

CHAPTER 6

Welcome To Hell – Also Known As Entering The Workforce

Staring at the elevator door, my hands shook. I hated driving downtown, and I despised what I was about to do: Walk in and start a job as the assistant to Rebecca Wilson, CPA. The situation was made worse by the pounding hangover.

After returning home from book club on Friday, I'd spent most of the weekend in the water, glass of wine always nearby. Screw the housework. The choices were simple: Pool during the heat of day; hot tub when the air turned cooler at night. Carol joined me for a while Friday night, laughing and giggling with me, celebrating my new job with "crazy Aunt Becca" and dishing on her afternoon at orientation, until her fingers shriveled.

"See, Mom? I told you: we're all here to help you. You'll be so busy working, you won't even notice when I leave for school. I'm really glad I'm going to be close enough to come home on the weekends. You know, to bring home my dirty laundry and such? Eat real, homemade food?"

My daughter. She was my reason for living. Always had been, always would be, so the decision to lock up the beast inside me was made that night in the pool. The possibility was high that, after the last few weeks, I was moving away from being Wicked Witch of the West to Glinda.

The elevator doors opened and a rush of people crammed inside. Welcome to work life! Hurry, the moving sardine can is ready to take you up, up, *up* and away, depositing you at your joyous new job! Whoopee!

"Mrs. Davenport?"

The voice behind me was somewhat familiar. I tried turning around to put a face to the voice, but considering the elevator was packed with bodies, it was close to impossible. "Yes?"

"Huh, thought that was you," came the nervous reply.

Recognition of the voice slammed into my mind. Seriously? My very first day at work and I run into Hottie Habanero? My luck sucked dirty balls and Carl's are nowhere in sight! Of course she worked in the same building! Of course she did!

Oh. My. God! I'd be forced to see her every day! And Carl! What in the hell would I do if Carl came to have lunch with her and I saw them together? Jesus, it's really hot in this elevator. Really. Freaking. Warm. Hot flash? Panic attack? Mental breakdown?

Yep, all three rolled into one.

I knew the job was a mistake the second Rebecca's lips uttered the words. Being a part of the workforce was not in my comfort zone and not my cup of tea. I was out of my element among the metal and glass buildings, the heavy traffic, and the loud noises. I belonged on tree-lined streets where the sidewalks were filled with dogs, children, and other mothers toting their offspring to the park, or waiting at the curb's edge for the ice cream truck. Homeroom mother; Girl Scout troupe leader; cheering face in the stands at any and all school events—that was my role in life.

I didn't belong here, and confirmation of my gut instincts was only feet away.

I wonder how many rules I'd break if I pulled out a cigarette and lit up? Did I care? Hell no! My soon-to-be-ex's baby mama was right behind me! If arrested for lighting up, surely there'd be some sort of grace passed along for dealing with such unreal craziness!

The doors opened and in a rush to escape, I tripped and fell, purse flying, contents sliding across the slick marble floor of Baxter, Baxter, & Jenson, CPAs. Fuck! Bet ol H.H. was cracking up on her way to the next floor.

"Are you okay?"

Looking up, I frowned. "Yes, I'm fine Ms. Holloway. Don't let my clumsiness interrupt you on your way to wherever you work."

Bending down to retrieve a tube of lipstick, Ginger said: "It's no problem. I'm at work."

Stunned, I stuttered: "What … you … work here?"

Handing me the lipstick, Ginger nodded. "Yes, but only for two more weeks. I, uh, well, Carl got me a job at the university."

Stars danced in front of my eyes. A rush of memories hit me like the proverbial freight train.

Rebecca's casual remark about needing Mom's house soon.

The out-of-the-blue job offer.

L.B.'s insistence I start Monday, rather than wait until the divorce was final.

Why Ginger assumed I was the maid—and how she got our home address.

My loving, supportive, twatwaffle sister sent ol' Hottie to my house, knowing damn well the girl was pregnant with Carl's baby.

Something inside my mind snapped, just like it did when little, and Rebecca and I fought. Instead of torturing her baby dolls, it was time to unleash my rage on a real person. I'd been angry with Carl, but I was beyond infuriated at Rebecca's ultimate betrayal.

Welcome to the apocalypse.

"You work for Rebecca Wilson, right?" I asked Ginger through clenched teeth. My voice sounded odd, distant, like it was coming from an ancient set of speakers.

"Yes, how did you know that?" Ginger gasped.

Fuck the remaining items from my purse. I had my wallet,

keys, and phone, so the rest could stay put. Rising to my feet, I didn't even look at Ginger. "Because she's my sister, and believe it or not, I'm supposed to be your replacement."

"Supposed?" Ginger asked.

Turning back to face H.H., I scowled. "I just started and quit in the space of one second. You should probably wait out here, Ms. Holloway, while I go have a little chat with my precious sister. Better yet, seek shelter. Ignorant bystanders tend not to survive the apocalypse."

My heart beat so fast my chest hurt. Never, in my entire life, had I been so furious. While tromping down the hallway leading to Rebecca's plush corner office, everything seemed coated in a red haze. Like in movies when someone is on drugs or suffers a blow to the head, my visual perception was skewed. The office looked odd, as though walking through a weird, tilted maze.

I didn't acknowledge any of the staff as I strode toward Rebecca's door. The faint sounds of their voices, including Ginger's worried one, barely registered.

I was on a mission. A mission to beat the living shit out of my sister. Our roles were now swapped; I was the lunatic bitch.

Rebecca's door was closed so I flung it open. Sitting at her fancy desk, decked out in a red power suit, enhanced cleavage peeking out from a low-cut white dress shirt, a set of overpriced, designer reading glasses perched on her nose, Rebecca let out a small, fake gasp.

"Roxy? What's wrong?"

Rather than respond with words, I picked up my pace, fist and arm at the ready. Rebecca had just enough time to stand before I released my anger right into her face.

Pow!

Fist to the nose.

Blood burst from the explosion of my fury. The force of the punch knocked Rebecca to the floor, sending piles of paper in the air and spilling a cup of coffee all over the desk. I heard someone scream and another call for security. I didn't care. I'd be arrested for sure, once the fat, slow assholes assigned to protect the building made it up to the thirtieth floor.

But not before I unleashed a world of hurt on Rebecca.

Blood poured from in between her fingers as she covered her nose. Scooting away, she tried to stand up, but I was on her before she had the chance.

Bending down, I grabbed a handful of her over-processed blonde hair and extensions, raised her head just enough to land a solid connection with her eye socket.

Smack!

Yeow! Bone on bone smarts!

"You … fucking … bitch!" I yelled while landing blows with each word. "How could you do this to me? To Carol?"

To my surprise, Rebecca wasn't crying, or cowering in fear. Instead of being afraid, I realized she was actually laughing. Okay, so she still retained the moniker of Lunatic Bitch, because only a crazy person would cackle like a sick rooster while getting their ass beat.

"Mrs. Wilson? Are you okay?" a man's voice yelled from the doorway. "Should I call the police?"

The distraction gave Rebecca the opportunity to kick my feet out from under me. I landed hard on my ass right next to her, a handful of her hair still clasped in my fingers.

"I'm fine. Family shit. Shut the door and let us be, Dwight. It's all over now."

Rebecca scrambled to her feet, a trail of blood and spit left in her wake. I heard the door shut, grabbed hold of a thin ankle, and twisted. L.B. toppled over, and in a flash, I was on top of her, fingers firmly intertwined in her hair.

"Why?" I asked, followed by slamming her head into the floor. "Why, Rebecca? You're my sister!"

"Stop smacking me around and I'll gladly share, Roxy. Gladly. I've been waiting a long time for this conversation."

"You're certifiable," I hissed.

"Wrong. You are," Rebecca responded, letting go of her destroyed nose and latching her fingers around my throat.

Rolling around on the expensive flooring like two crazy women, Rebecca and I fought it out. Hair flew. Fingernails broke. Blood littered the floor. For the most part, I had the upper hand, clawing, kicking, punching the crap out of my mean-as-fuck sister. The fight ended with white hot pain and me gasping for air on the floor, after the bitch's bony knee connected with my pelvic bone.

(Side note—yes, men crumple into worthless heaps when their twigs and berries take a blow. Though perhaps not as painful to women as when a man takes a whack to the nads, a solid, bony knee hurts like hell when it connects with the vagina. We see stars, too).

Groaning, hands clamped between my throbbing legs, I couldn't do a thing except listen to Rebecca stand and walk to her desk. I heard her rummaging around, wondering if she was searching for a letter opener or some other sharp object to finish me off with.

"You asked why, so here's the answer, dear Roxy. It was time to dethrone you as Queen Bee of Cherrywood Estates. It's my turn to take over. Oh, and I hate you."

Rolling over to my back, the stars in my vision slowly disappearing, I responded: "Yeah, well the feeling's mutual, but still doesn't explain why you did it."

"You don't have any idea what it's like to live in your shadow. I've spent my whole life being compared to the great Roxy Rayburn! Jesus, I can't count how many times I heard I needed to be more like you. Not just from Mom or Dad, but teachers, friends, and my fucking spouse."

Crawling toward the couch in the corner, I grimaced. "What does Stephen have to do with our feud?"

"Everything! The minute we met, though I don't think he realized he was doing it, he compared me to you. I worked my ass off to be better, and much more successful, than you. Make people see me rather than Roxy's little sister. Didn't work."

"Make sense, will you?" I muttered, finally on the couch.

"You lived the perfect life, Roxy. A family; beautiful house; perfect child. The great Roxy was always gorgeous, and people, including my husband, drooling over you. Everyone around you tried to mimic every move you made so they could be more like you. When I saw how Mom and Dad rallied around you when you got knocked up and dropped out of school, I even tried to do the same. Again, it didn't work. I sucked it up though, and just kept pushing myself, forcing all my energy into my career. I don't have children from lack of trying, I assure you. I wanted your life, but my lady parts had other ideas."

"So, because you're a barren bitch, you decided to ruin my life?"

"No, that decision came from a conversation with Stephen the day I found out Ginger was Carl's newest squeeze."

Stunned, I looked across the room at Rebecca. She was a mess, but still wore an air of superiority like a trophy. "Wait a minute—you only called to make sure I was home, right? No wonder the courier never showed up! Are you saying—?"

"Yes, to both. I didn't know about the two of them until Ginger ran in here, crying her eyes out. She thought the baby was her boyfriend's, not Carl's. Just to be safe, since she'd been screwing them both, she made them each get tested. To say she wasn't thrilled with the results is an understatement. She whined and cried, going on and on about how the old man, Professor Davenport—who, by the way, she only screwed to get a better grade—was the father. The part about Mom's house is true— I just haven't gotten around to doing it yet. Other things dropped into my lap, requiring all my attention."

"You saw the opportunity to hurt me and ran with it, right?"

Rebecca tossed the wad of bloody tissues into the trash can by her desk. "No, you fool! I was genuinely upset and shocked, okay, and I'll admit, a part of me found it funny. I told Ginger to go wash up and calm down then I called Stephen. I had to tell him, ask for advice about what I should do. His response is what made me decide to use the situation as the proverbial knife in the back."

"Stephen is too nice of a guy to come up with such a mean plan, Rebecca. I'm not buying into what you're selling."

"I didn't say it was his idea, bitch. I said his response gave me the idea. I had to listen to him go on and on about the awful situation, how the news would devastate 'poor Roxy' and how surprised he was Carl cheated on you, given the fact you're so 'gorgeous' and 'every man's dream.' Something inside me snapped, so when Ginger returned to my office, I gave her your address."

While catching my breath, listening to Rebecca spill her morbid reasons for destroying my life, I thought back to our younger years. All the times I'd teased her mercilessly, picked on her for one silly reason or another. Remembered some of the more vicious pranks I'd played on her, laughing when she'd scurry off to her room, crying like a baby. All the arguments about clothes, chores—typical sibling rivalry shit.

Did she know about her toys I'd tortured too?

No, I hadn't been a very kind older sister, so part of me understood Rebecca's anger. However, it's one thing to hold an old, sisterly grudge; quite another to wait for years for payback and do something so hurtful to a blood relative. I mean, it's not like I wouldn't have found out anyway about the baby, which probably would have opened up the can of worms about all the other women Carl bedded over the years, but that didn't matter to me. Rebecca used the situation to strike a mortal blow to our relationship, taking our rivalry to a whole new level.

Voices outside the door grew louder, and I sensed our little heart-to-heart was about to be interrupted with my arrest. Rising to my feet, ignoring the throbbing of my broken twat, I walked over and picked up my purse.

"Congratulations, L.B. You won this round, but here's a news-flash: I don't play by *The Suburbia Handbook* any longer. I burned that sucker into a pile of ashes. I live by a new set of rules now. Roxy's rules. And when the *real* Roxy comes out of the dark corners inside my mind, things get ugly. And painful. Fast. I'm giving you fair warning, dear sister; you'll pay for this betrayal. You won't know when, how, or see it coming, but trust me, it's on its way. By the time I'm through with you, you'll wish you were an only child."

Rebecca sneered, teeth and lips coated in blood. "I've wished that my entire life. Bring it, bitch. I'm not afraid of you one bit."

Standing her ground as I approached, our gazes locked. I stopped inches from Rebecca's torn-up face. Voice low and tone ominous, I whispered: "You should be."

Fear flashed for a split second in Rebecca's eyes, though she recovered quickly. She flipped me the bird, her go-to way of ending a conversation she no longer wished to participate in.

Pointing to her cell on the desk, I added: "Make sure to share a picture of your bloody face. Caption it 'Sibling Rivalry Never Ends' hashtag broken nose."

With the threat out in the open, I left, head held high, though walking a bit strangely, ignoring the stares of countless shocked employees of Baxter, Baxter & Jensen in my wake.

Once in the elevator, mind abuzz with dark thoughts, I realized the old Roxy was completely gone. Bits and pieces of her had been torn away by others, and the last remaining traces were obliterated by a family member. I didn't think about how the plans forming inside my mind would affect others, or the ramifications for actually carrying out the brutal thoughts.

No, the days of being a serene housewife were over. It was time to go home, grab my journal, and start planning my revenge.

Roxy's New Rule Number Nine: Make those who hurt me, pay. With blood.

CHAPTER 7

A Visit Goes Awry

I had to do something to calm down besides go home and drink until I blacked out. What I really wanted, more than anything in the world, was to talk to my father. He'd been the only person who really understood me and I could trust with all my secrets. Daddy knew things about me even my bestie didn't. Whatever the reason, whether it was because I was the firstborn or our personalities were so similar, we clicked. Two peas in a pod was the expression he'd always say. No one could soothe my nerves like Roger Rayburn, and boy, my nerves were way beyond frazzled. They were burnt to a crisp.

Why in the world did I even consider Rebecca was doing something nice for me out of consideration of our blood ties? Family bonds? It was really my fault what happened at Baxter, Baxter & Jensen, because I let my guard down, allowing my heart and mind an *Awww, how kind of my sister!* moment.

Never again would I be so incredibly stupid.

Ever.

Once I made it out of the parking deck, it was like I was on autopilot as I zoomed through downtown traffic. Rage and humiliation took over and I was helpless to stop them. The showdown with L.B. played over and over inside my mind. I'd unleashed my fury yet stopped before I killed her, and not just because the bitch busted my pussy.

No, I didn't continue the fight because I'd been dangerously close to committing murder, and it would have been a mistake to do so with so many witnesses around. I needed to calm down, think like a rational person and plan the perfect revenge for Rebecca Denise Rayburn Wilson, C. P. Fucking A.

In a haze, I was surprised when I found myself in the parking lot of Natalie's Nature Extravaganza, my favorite local nursery, staring at a display of vibrant ferns.

"Hey, Roxy! Oh, wow, what happened to you?"

How in the world did I forget about my injuries? Dammit! Think, Roxy. Come up with a believable story. I was so out of it I didn't even put my sunglasses on. "Oh, just a little outpatient nip tuck yesterday, you know? Doing my part to keep the age spots and wrinkles away."

"Thank goodness! Sorry, I wasn't trying to be rude but, for a second there, I thought maybe you'd been in a fight or something!"

My, the little hippie florist still had some brain cells left! The fake laughter from my lips sounded weird. "I'm a mother, not a fighter."

"Isn't the expression a lover not a fighter?"

I nodded, praying the little tree-hugger would shut the fuck up. I had things to do, dead people to visit, the downfall of L.B. to plan. "Ha! You're right. Guess I need more coffee to rev up my tired brain."

"I was hoping you'd stop by this week. I thought about calling you, yet decided I'd wait until you came by, after what happened. I got in some new roses yesterday. They're gorgeous and smell heavenly! I set back two for you. I thought you might like one for home and perhaps one for Rachel's, uh, graveside? I read her obituary in the paper last week. I'm so very sorry."

Looking at the beautiful, pale-pink rose bushes Natalie pointed at behind the counter, I forced a smile. "How thoughtful of you. I appreciate you thinking about me and Rachel. I'd like three, please. I'll need one each for the graves of Rachel and Dad, and one for my backyard."

"You bet!" Natalie chirped. In a flash, she had three gorgeous, healthy plants ready for me to take home. "It's a beautiful day to be outside with your fingers in the dirt. There isn't anything more relaxing than …"

Nodding in agreement at what I hoped were appropriate times, Natalie's words took a backseat in my mind. I had a raging headache, my vajajay still ached, and my entire body felt like, well, I'd been in a fight. Looking down at my clothes, thankful I had a sweater covering the bloodstains on my dress shirt, I shuddered.

I didn't remember putting it on or it even being in my car.

You're losing it, Roxanne.

The overwhelming urge to go sit by Daddy's grave and release my angst overrode common sense. I'd just bought three plants and didn't have a shovel or gardening gloves with me.

"Roxy? Did you hear me?"

Blinking twice, I stared at … shit, what's her name? My brain is so jacked at the moment I'm lucky I remember my own. "I'm sorry, no. I was just admonishing myself for neglecting to bring the proper tools I'll need to plant these. I'll have to drive all the way back home. What did you say?"

"That'll be $65.50. And don't you worry, girl. Grief does that sometimes. When I lost my mom, I forgot to take my birth control pills for weeks, which is how Aiden arrived. My husband was so surprised. He said, 'Natalie, what were you thinking?' I told him I wasn't because I was in mourning. Anyway, enough about me. If you need some gardening stuff, how about I throw in a shovel and a set of gloves? On the house as my way of saying thank you for being such a loyal customer."

"Again, very kind of you. Thanks." I handed her seventy bucks in cash then scooped up three plants and headed to the car. "Keep the change."

Minutes later, trunk crammed with the purchases, a wave of dizziness hit me.

"Roxy? Are you okay? You look like you're about to pass out! Maybe you should have waited another day after surgery before venturing out?"

Sucking in a lungful of fragrant air, I put on my best smile. "I'm sure that's not it. I forgot to eat breakfast this morning and I guess my body's rebelling. I'll be fine. Thank you again for being so kind. Life's been rough the last few weeks. It's nice to know some good, kindhearted souls are still around."

A warm hand touched my elbow and helped guide me to the driver's door. "I'm really sorry about Rachel, Roxy. Truly. Like I said before the best way I've found in dealing with life's difficult moments is to dig a hole, plant a new life, and bury the pain inside my soul right next to the roots. Works like a charm. Oh, and some stout skunk to help ease a stressed mind and calm a rumbling gut. I'd be willing to—"

"No, thank you. I don't smoke pot. Only cigarettes." Considering the way things have gone during the last few weeks, perhaps I should reconsider? Light up and float away on a cloud of THC? Puff away on the magic dragon since I wouldn't have Raging Rufus to contend with any longer? Trade my wine glasses in for a pipe or bong? Nah. I'm a wino not a midnight toker. Besides, who wants to smell like a freaking skunk rather than fruity grapes?

"You sure? Medicinal marijuana is legal now. All you have to do is call your doctor and get a prescription. Weed is much better for you than Xanax or Ambien."

"Yes, I'm aware, but again, I only enjoy nicotine. Thanks for the good advice about planting. I'll see you in a few weeks when it's time to replace my petunias," I responded, afraid any second I'd pull a Linda Blair and spew chunks all over Natalie's face.

Once back on the road, I wound my way through the side

streets until at the back entrance of Eternal Slumber Acres. The space was tucked away behind a huge grove of evergreen trees on the outskirts of the county.

Back in its heyday, nearly a century ago, the fifty-acre spread had been spectacular. Remnants of the opulence could be seen in the ornate headstones, the thick, wrought iron fence nearly twelve feet high surrounding the property, and the marble serenity benches dotting the walking trails.

Upon closer inspection, years of neglect surfaced. The headstones were cracked, faded and dull, along with the serenity benches, most of which were in such deplorable condition sitting on them would be a risky choice. The gate still stood, yet instead of shiny ebony, a gray sheen covered large sections that weren't already rusted out. The concrete on the walking trails was dirty, stained from countless feet stepping on them and years upon years of rain beating down. What remained really wasn't concrete. It was more like crushed rocks held together by hardened, green slime.

I killed the engine in the empty parking lot, looking around the tranquil place, wishing someone had come to cut the weeds down. Vines and kudzu wound around sections of the fence and numerous trees, and some of the weeds by the edges of the fence seemed to have grown a foot since Rachel's funeral.

Stepping out of the car, I popped the trunk and retrieved the rose bushes, shovel, and gloves, which fit perfectly. Nails covered, heart and soul ready, I picked up the first bush, mindful of the thorns, and headed toward the back of the corner lot, where my departed loved ones rested on the other side of a small berm.

Other than the faint rustle of leaves from a light breeze, it was quiet. The graves were so old, most of the loved ones of the departed were probably dead as well, so no one came to visit the plots. Not one headstone, as far as I could see, sported any flowers.

Mom and Dad purchased plots for the entire family—how

fucking *morbid* is that?—not long after Rachel was born. Daddy told me, once, they got them for a real bargain, since the five plots were the last spaces available, which meant "the Rayburn clan" would be the final interred residents of Eternal Slumber Acres.

Two of them were already sleeping, and I feared Mom would be the third by the end of the year.

How in the world would I handle the loss?

No, I wouldn't think about losing Mom. I couldn't. Too much was already on my mind.

It was time to visit—Dad first so I could dump out my mental baggage, and then Rachel. Say what's on my mind then plant the roses.

Dammit. I forgot the shovel and to lock my car. Though there wasn't a soul around, at least not anyone alive, it was better to be safe than sorry. Eternal Slumber Acres was in the sticks, miles from the city, and after the morning I'd had, it was best not to push my luck. Wouldn't it just be dandy if some weirdo was lurking in the woods and stole my car? The thought of walking all the way home made my twat throb.

Setting down the rose bush, I turned and went back to the car.

Then, shovel in hand, car secured and keys in my pocket, I headed back to the trail. Maybe I'd feel better and could finally calm down once the bushes were planted and—

I froze mid-stride.

The buzzing was back inside my head.

Maybe it was the bright morning sun playing tricks on me? It had to be because, good Lord, how much more drama could a person handle in one fucking day?

No, maybe I'm wrong. Perhaps the cemetery finally hired a caretaker and he's starting the cleaning process at the newest grave. It can't be him!

Bypassing the rose bush sitting on the path, I stepped into the soft grass and kept walking. Once about ten feet away, confirmation of the unwanted visitor was made.

What the hell? The boy had a lot of nerve showing up here!

He heard my steps and stood, facing me. "Hello, Roxy."

The look on his face and ominous tone made me shiver. He had to be on some type of drug because his words were slurred, and I swear he was still wearing the same outfit he'd had on at the funeral. Dirty and disheveled, his rank body odor drifted across the space between us. Stopping, I gave him a sour look. "What are you doing here, Benny?"

"What do you think, bitch? I came to finish saying my goodbyes since you made me leave the service before I had a chance to say my piece. Took me a few days to make it here because I've been looking for work. My, uh, financial situation recently took a downturn."

Did he just call me bitch and allude to the fact he was using Rachel for money or am I hallucinating? God, please let me be hallucinating.

Taking a step forward, a demented smirk crossed his thin lips. "What's wrong, big sis? Not as bold when you're all alone and don't have an audience to show off in front of, huh?"

I started shaking, but it wasn't from fear.

It was from fury.

The boy had no idea he was poking a hornet's nest. "Leave, right now," I hissed.

Benny eased closer. "Yep, you're scared, as you should be. You had the upper hand before when you, let's see, what did you threaten to do to me again? Oh yeah, slice my balls off. My, what would little Rachel say if she heard her big sister say such ugly things to the man she loved? She'd probably tell you to mind your own business and leave us be. Damn, I sure do miss her. She gave great head. Guess I shouldn't have told her to wait and let her body heal itself rather than going to the hospital. Stupid mistake. Live and learn, right?"

No. You. Didn't.

Planting my feet, I raised the shovel like a baseball bat, ready to swing for the outfield. "One more word and I'll bash your freaking skull in and bury you."

"Oh, I'm so scared!" Benny roared with laughter. "Go ahead, I dare you! Better get a good lick in though, because if you don't take me down with the first one, I'm going to make you wish you'd never crossed me. You look pretty good for an old broad. I'm curious about how you taste."

Wrong choice of words, Benny-Boo.

Benny lunged.

Wrong choice again.

My touch with sanity broke as red filled my vision.

Soon, it wasn't just an optical illusion as the *whack whack whack* of the shovel connecting with flesh and bone filled the late morning air.

CHAPTER 8

Rambling Dreams Of A Crazed Housewife

By the time I arrived home, I was unnaturally calm, which was beyond odd. Shouldn't I be hysterical? Panicked? Terrified any second the cops would knock on my door and haul me away for killing the sack of shit, leaving his body as rose food? Where was the shred of remorse for taking the life of another human being?

Oh yeah, I lost it the night I let the *real* me come out to play with Carl.

Yes, I should be all those things, and more, yet I wasn't.

Not at all.

After hiding my deed, I drove through the streets with a smile plastered on my face, mindful of the speed limit, all my attention completely focused on the task of driving.

I never shook once or shed a single tear.

If, by a slim chance, someone ever discovered Mr. Environmentally Friendly's remains buried inches above Rachel's casket, with a fresh rose bush planted on top, tying it to me would be difficult. The only person who knew I'd gone to the cemetery was Natalie, and since most of the time she was so stoned she couldn't remember her name, it was doubtful she'd even recall our visit. I paid with cash, so if my bank account was ever searched there would be no evidence I'd been at her store. No one had seen me at the cemetery; Benny had no close family—according to Rachel—and I wore gloves the entire time.

He didn't have a car, so he walked or rode the bus everywhere (or relied on others, like Rachel when she was alive, to tote him around) which meant there wasn't a vehicle to be found at the cemetery. The streaks of blood on my clothes wouldn't matter—I'd burned them down to nothing but a pile of ashes in the fireplace, along with the sheepskin cover from the front seat, just to be safe if any blood transferred from my clothes. The bleach and oxidizer I used to clean the interior of my car surely wiped away most of the traces of his blood, and I'd repeat the same cleaning every day for a week just to make sure, in case the cosmos shit on me.

Again.

No one would ever know, except me, about the dirty little secret at Eternal Slumber Acres. If someone ever reported the loser missing, no one would think to dig up Rachel's grave and search for his body.

Free and clear, baby.

Could I live with the fact I killed someone without going insane?

Hell yes! I did the world a favor by ridding it of the lazy bastard! The fool attacked me first after running off his filthy mouth about Rachel, plus ruined what might have been a memorable visit with Dad. After all, it's not like I planned to kill Benny; it was an accident. I had no idea he'd be skulking around Rachel's grave then attempt to harm me.

Self-defense, baby.

A demerit hovered over my head for not informing the authorities, yet I pretended it wasn't there. Benny broke a rule and deserved to be punished, right? Isn't that how a civilized society is supposed to work? Step out of bounds and pay the price? Hmm,

I doubt that would fly since it was my personal rule he broke, but I didn't care.

The only thing that bothered me about what happened was Carol. If she ever found out what I'd done, she would freak out. Though she loved her aunt Rachel, I doubt she'd approve of me killing Benny, even if I told her exactly how things went down between us.

I'd just make sure she never did.

"I'll think about that tomorrow," I whispered, doing my best impression of Scarlett O'Hara.

How befitting we were at a cemetery and a grave close by? Ol' Benny-Boo would contribute to making a small section of the world a beautiful place as his rotting flesh fed the plants around it.

Good. Fucking. Riddance. No one would miss his nasty ass anyway.

***

Once I finished getting rid of the evidence, I headed upstairs, took a shower, washed, and pampered my sore vagina and then went downstairs to the dining room table. It was close to noon, which meant it was socially acceptable to start drinking. Wine at the ready, I began to write.

After several hours of scribbling, the journal had ten more pages added to it, planning the downfall of Rebecca Denise Rayburn Wilson. Ugly, hateful words scribbled across the pages in bright, blue ink, adding a few tweaks to the demise of others. The only thing I didn't write down was my little side venture at the cemetery.

Honestly, I didn't want to relive those dark moments.

By the time I'd plotted out the deaths of several people, the full bottle of Moscato was empty and my head spinning.

It was close to four, which meant Carol would arrive home any minute. My drunken mind wanted to continue on with the dark ramblings, but the mom in me wouldn't allow any more, at least, not until after Carol went to bed.

***

My fingers ached so I decided to give them a break. Standing, I stretched then made a loop of the downstairs rooms. Everything was familiar, all the furniture, decorations, memorabilia of the Davenport household—same as usual, yet it all seemed wrong. Foreign. Like my entire existence had been a weird dream I just woke up from.

A cheating husband.

Dead sister and father.

Absent mother.

Treacherous, hateful sibling.

Knocked-up neighbors and whores.

A sore twat.

A daughter leaving home.

A life torn to pieces.

"This isn't my house." I belted out the rest of the song by the Talking Heads while wobbling to the kitchen. A space stocked with expensive, shiny appliances, top-notch accessories, and the latest style. The lovely area had been a birthday gift from Carl two years before. "He isn't my husband," I continued to sing, altering the words to suit my pathetic life.

Staring at the fridge, my mind was blank in terms of what to fix. It needed to be something easy, because in my current state of inebriation, I might hurt myself with cutlery or fire.

"Soup and sandwiches tonight, Carol. Sorry."

After preparing the pathetic dinner, I contemplated grabbing another bottle of wine, yet hesitated. I was already woozy, and didn't need to be thoroughly trashed before Carol arrived home. I'd save that experience for later, while I continued to kill off my enemies inside the pages of the journal.

One *real* killing was enough for the day, but there was no limit on *fictional* deaths.

My cell buzzed on the counter. Carol's assigned ringtone. Snatching it up, I read the text: "*Dad asked me to dinner to talk so I'm going be home later don't wait up luv ya!*"

"Motherfucker! Not tonight! I need you here, Carol, or I'll break. Do things you'll hate me for later."

Another text, this time from Liz: "*So how was the first day? Did you two try to kill each other? Details, woman. I want details. Call when you can.*"

Mind spinning, terrified of what I might do if left alone, I called for backup. "Liz? Can you come over?"

Hearing the stress in my voice, Liz responded: "Oh, shit. That bad, huh?"

"Yeah, I need to talk."

"Let me finish dinner and I'll be right over. Ten minutes, tops."

"Bring wine. I'm almost out."

"I already bought two bottles earlier. Sort of figured today would be hard on you. Be there in a flash."

Hanging up, I smiled. Liz was the best friend ever in the history of best friends, which made exposing the ugly secrets, the pent-up rage, even harder. Taking a deep breath, I turned off the stove and dumped the soup down the sink. (Demerit—wasting food!) I took a bit of comfort in the fact I would unleash the truth to Liz's ears, and not Carol's.

Because honestly, after today, I didn't know how much longer it would be before something bad, something really bad, happened—to a *lot* of people.

"Roxy! What happened? Did you have a wreck downtown? Are you okay?"

Liz rushed over next to me, examining my face. She was so shocked by my appearance she almost dropped the wine bottles.

"Yeah, had a wreck all right. Ran into a freight train named Raging Rebecca."

"You … what? Oh, shit, wait a second. Let me get you some ice. Your eye looks awful. That's going to be a hell of a shiner. Sure you don't need stitches on your lip?"

"I'm fine, Liz. Promise."

Rushing to the kitchen, I heard Liz fumble around, ice clinking, fridge door slamming. In seconds she was back with a dish towel full of ice. After handing it to me, she opened a bottle and poured two full glasses.

"Thanks, sweetie," I muttered.

"I knew working for her was a bad idea. How long did it last before the fighting started?"

"Oh, about three seconds. Never even made it to my desk."

Furrowing her brows in confusion, Liz asked: "What the hell happened? I mean, I know you two aren't close, but this? A freaking fist fight? The last time you two went at each other was what—when we were in ninth grade? Hope she looks worse than you do."

"She does. Ol' L.B.'s going to need surgery on her nose again. I broke it. Oh, and a trip to the salon. I yanked out about five hundred dollars' worth of extensions."

"Good for you. The burning question is why?"

Downing a huge gulp of wine, I sighed. "I haven't told you a lot of things that happened recently, and until I do, our fight won't make much sense."

"Spill. I'm here, and ready to listen. I have a sneaking suspicion this has something to do with Carl. You're about to tell me he screwed Rebecca, aren't you?"

I laughed. The images of my uptight sister banging Carl, his itchy belly making her complain the entire time, were comical. "I wouldn't beat her up for that. I'd insist she go get tested for STDs."

"What? I don't understand?"

"I'll try my best to explain, but it'll be difficult since I'm still grappling with the whole nightmare. I assume, based on your comment, you won't be shocked to learn Carl cheated on me."

Liz closed her eyes, dread spreading across her beautiful face. "No, I wouldn't. I've seen the way he looks at other women. Plus, in the past, you've mentioned his addiction to porn. Not really surprising he took the next step."

"No, guess not. I was just a blind fool for years," I sighed, taking another drink. "Let's head out back. I need nicotine to continue this conversation."

"Okay. I'll bring the wine."

Once situated out by the pool, feet hanging over the edge in the cool water, I let the words pour out of me. I told my best friend everything, except about the journal of murder stashed away and what I did at the cemetery. Tears welled up in her eyes when I told her about the visit from Hottie Habanero, then her emotions switched over to hysterical laughter when I got to the part about Carl's night of punishment. Liz gasped then laughed right along with me, actually suggesting I write the entire experience on paper and maybe publish it as a short story. Other women who'd been married to cheating spouses would devour the tale. A few times, Liz simply gaped at me with wide eyes, stunned by the violence. At one point, she almost looked frightened.

The laughter ended when I got to the part about Coco, and my fears she'd been carrying Carl's baby, and how I freaked at book club.

After I finished with what went down at Baxter, Baxter, & Jensen, Liz was tipsy, and she'd been so shocked, she almost fell into the pool.

Twice.

"I just—wow, I don't even know what to say. This shit doesn't even happen in Lifetime movies! I mean, it just *can't* be real! No wonder you haven't been your smiling self lately!"

"I'm right there with you, girl. Right there with you. It was hard enough dealing with what happened to Rachel, but all this, too? I'm losing my marbles."

Putting a warm arm around my shoulder, Liz responded: "That's why you have me around, to keep you from going insane. We'll get through this. Promise. First item on the agenda is what to tell Carol. When she gets home, she's going to ask how your day went, after she freaks when seeing your face. Are you going to tell her the truth?"

"How can I? She's just a child! Carol can't handle these things."

"Roxy, she's 18. Leaving for college soon. You raised her right. Taught her to be strong, independent. Give her some credit. Her reaction might surprise you."

"I'm a grown woman and I can barely handle all this shit. How do I tell my daughter she's about to be an older sister? That her father is a sick freak, one who got his rocks off from porn and younger women? Dump all that onto her young shoulders, then add in what her aunt did? No. No way."

"Okay, I get that. You want to shield her from the painful knowledge her father is a pile of dog shit. Got it. Let her find out later about the impending sibling, maybe from Carl's lips and not yours. But, how are you going to explain your face? The fact you aren't working with Rebecca? What are you going to do if Rebecca gets to her first and drops the news?"

Anger rumbled inside my chest. "She wouldn't dare!"

"Wouldn't she? After what she did already, I don't put it past her. She's a vindictive twat."

"That she is, Liz. No doubt. But, her beef was with me, and she loves Carol. Rebecca wouldn't do anything to hurt her."

Liz's eyebrow raised in disbelief. "Uh, wrong. She started this entire mess by sending, oh, what did you call her again?"

"Hottie Habanero."

"Yep, that's it! Rebecca knew exactly what would happen after sending Hottie Habanero over here. By hurting you, Rebecca hurt Carol by proxy. I don't think you should keep the truth from her.

It's going to be painful, but hearing it from your mouth, instead of someone else's, will be easier. I think. Shit, I don't know. I could be wrong. Advice is always easier when dispensing it, not taking it. If our roles were swapped, I'm not sure I'd be able to tell Richard."

"I'm not going to do anything tonight. I'm too exhausted. After a good night's sleep, and a chance for the swelling to go down, I'll figure out what to do in the morning. Thanks for listening to me bare my soul, Liz. I do feel better. Sort of."

It took a few seconds for both of us to stand. Liz was trashed, and I was quite buzzed. "Let me help you to bed, sweetie. I don't want you falling down the stairs."

"Oh! Idea! I could always tell Carol I fell down them after drinking too much. You know, I came home from a long day at work, knocked a few too many back, busted my ass?"

While leaning against each other for support, Liz laughed. "Believable? No doubt. The right thing to do? No. One lie always leads to more. Now, stop thinking and get some rest. Tomorrow things will be clearer, and you'll make the right choice. I know you will."

Wobbling up the stairs, mind way past the point of sanity, I didn't respond. I let Liz tuck me in, hanging on to the edges of the comforter as waves of dizziness overtook me. Liz's warm lips pressed against my forehead, followed by a low murmur of love before she left my bedroom.

I tried to stay awake, waiting for the sound of Carol's VW, but blackness swooped in, carrying my mind away to dark, disturbing dreams.

***

Bus. I'm riding the bus at night—in the dangerous big city! Shit! I hate being downtown. No, wait, no longer on the bus. Dark. It's really dark, not one star or beam of moonlight in the sky.

The air is cold, and goosebumps pepper my entire body as I walk, alone, through an unfamiliar alleyway.

Something cold and hard is in my hand. Raising my arm for a better look, I wince.

A knife. A blood-soaked kitchen knife.

Stopping short, I gasp. My hand is covered in crimson. Heart pounding, I spin around, trying to figure out my location. The sounds of the city greet my ears, and the faintest glimmer of light from a streetlamp in the distance sparks to life. Looking down, I notice the black leggings and sweater sport the same, sticky red mess.

Oh. My. God. What have I done? Where am I? Whose blood is this?

Running. I'm running as dirty bricks and the damp ground zoom by while I escape the alleyway. Images of crouching in a closet, waiting, holding my breath while watching and listening to my prey argue. The blood. All the fucking blood after I burst from my hiding spot, slashing and slicing through soft flesh.

My street. I'm on my street, clinging to the shadows while my friends and neighbors sleep. Tapping on a bedroom window. Now, I'm inside an unfamiliar bedroom, forcing myself not to laugh while shoving sleeping pills down the throat of my next victim, holding her still until the convulsions stopped. Dead. She's dead. One quick, deep slice into the arm, guiding a blood-soaked finger on the headboard, spelling out *I'm a home-wrecking whore* above the bed.

Carl's blood. Ginger's blood. Coco's blood.

Their dead eyes staring up into the ceiling, the floor and bed covered in pools of red.

Laughter. I hear laughter bouncing all around me. Sick, twisted laughter, full of madness and terror as sirens blare in the distance.

My laughter.

Sirens coming for me.

I'd just sliced and diced my ex and two of his whores.

Oh, shit.

Run, Roxy. Run! Get home, clean up, destroy the evidence. No, not that way! The cops are over there. Hurry! Don't let them see you. Stay away from the streetlamp!

Dammit! I'm too late. They're closing in. Don't say a word when they catch you.

Lawyer up.

***

Jerking awake, my body soaked in sweat and heart racing, a scream on the tip of my tongue, I scrambled to the bathroom. After throwing up, I went to the sink, tossing handfuls of cold water all over my sore face. Yikes, I did have a shiner. An ugly, bluish-black one, along with a split lip turning red. Infection. I should have listened to Liz and gotten stitches.

Shit.

"Calm down, girl. It was just a dream. See? No blood. No bloody clothes in the hamper. Home. I'm at home, and I never left. A horrifying nightmare caused by too much wine, the death of Benny, and too many angry words written. Not a good combination before bed."

"Mom? You okay?"

Startled by Carol's voice from the hallway, I jumped. "Yeah, I just had a nightmare, that's all. Be down in a second to fix your breakfast."

"It's okay, I already did. I know you've got to get ready for work too. I'm going in early today, so I should get off work around three. How about I fix spaghetti for dinner, have it ready when you get home? I want to hear all about your new job with Aunt Becca."

"Sure, baby. See you later," I answered.

"Love you! Have a good day."

Yep, I was close to melt down, because I swear I just heard my petulant child say she loved me and planned on fixing dinner. Oh! I'm Glinda! Yippee!

Wait—was it possible? Is my daughter doing drugs? Could her peppy demeanor be from a chemical alteration to her bloodstream? Nah, no way. Not my Carol. She wouldn't even take over-the-counter cramp medication, much less an aspirin. Carol Claire Davenport steered clear of pharmaceuticals. On rare occasions, like the death of her favorite aunt, she'd have a few glasses of wine, but that was it.

The conclusion for Carol's sweet demeanor: She was trying to show some kindness to her mother who was going through a difficult time. God, I love that girl.

Piling half a tube of toothpaste onto the brush, I scrubbed the nasty bile taste from my mouth then padded over to the window. Sure enough, Carol emerged from the front door, her long, beautiful black hair pulled back into a perfect bun, dressed in cute scrubs for work. She jumped into her car, cranked the speakers up, and zoomed out of the driveway.

The bright morning sun made me wince, so I closed the drape and went back to the bathroom. After freshening up, I headed down to the kitchen to fix some much-needed coffee.

While waiting for the first cup, something out of place on the counter caught my attention. The journal! Holy shit, I thought I put it away before Liz arrived? Ugh! Flipping it open, I added a new rule:

Roxy's New Rule Number Ten: Keep journal in a safe place, and make sure to return it to the same spot, even when drunk!

Stomach churning at the thought of anyone reading my murderous thoughts, I forced the bile back down. If someone read them, the men in white coats would come and haul me off to the looney bin for sure! The theme song "They're Coming to Take Me Away," from Dr. Demento thrummed inside my head. *Hoo-hoo, hee-hee, ha-ha!*

"Okay, where should I hide you that I won't forget and Carol would never look? Ah-ha! A perfect spot!"

Opening the door to the laundry room, a place my daughter was highly allergic to and no one ever entered other than me, I hid the journal behind the iron and spray starch, way in the back. Hopefully, I'd remember where I put it later, because once the hangover eased up and some coffee and nicotine flooded my system, I planned on finishing my devious plans to ruin Lunatic Bitch's life.

No death for my sister. The rage I wanted to unleash on her had been transferred over to Benny. Uh-uh. Death was too easy; over too quick. Nope, I planned on making her feel the same pain I did, and giving her visuals to haunt her the rest of her life, just like me. After all, she said she wanted to be like me, right? I was simply being a caring, older sister, making sure to help the younger sibling achieve her life's goals.

Hee hee.

Dr. Stephen Wilson, according to L.B., had an unhealthy infatuation with his sister-in-law. I planned on exploiting that, then videotaping our little tryst. Prepare the video then throw my sister a huge party, invite all her friends, our neighbors, even coworkers, for her upcoming birthday.

An over-the-top party featuring a special screening of *Roxy Fucked My Husband.* In Dolby surround sound and high definition, of course.

Ah, yes. Revenge is sweet, especially in the digital age.

CHAPTER 9

Unraveling At The Seams

After cleaning the interior of the car again, I went back inside and called my brother-in-law to set up a meeting to plan a surprise party for Rebecca at my house the next week. When Stephen answered, I was worried, wondering if Rebecca had told the hubster what happened at work. My concerns disappeared when Stephen mentioned he loved the idea of a surprise party for his wife, given the fact she'd experienced the terror of being mugged the day before.

Liar, liar, pants on fucking fire! Demerit! Nice lie, Rebecca!

Stephen never alluded to my short career at Baxter, Baxter, & Jensen, so I assumed his bitch wife never shared her devious plans with him. Figures. Rebecca was an entirely different creature around Stephen. Sweet, charming, doting to the point of servitude. Ol' L.B. hid her real, nasty side, saving it up and unleashing it on everyone else when Stephen wasn't close by.

Oh, I am so going to enjoy doing this, for a variety of reasons. Watching Rebecca's reactions was the best part. Idea! Make sure to take a video of Rebecca *watching* the sex tape between spouse and sister and then email it to her for later viewing. Help her relive the fun, in case she drinks too much and forgets the birthday party from Hell.

Score!

Screwing Stephen was another enjoyable part of my twisted idea. Out of all the husbands in Cherrywood Estates, Dr. Stephen Wilson was the hunk. Tall, lanky, with thick, blond hair, solid shoulders, and nice legs from daily runs around the neighborhood. Stephen possessed a firm, rounded ass, and bonus—a hairless belly in great shape.

Mmm, this was going to benefit me in so many ways!

I hadn't experienced the pleasure of a new dick in almost twenty years (unless you count a rubber one with batteries—faster, less messy, and no required assurances after you "got there"). True to my old nature, I'd remained faithful to ol' Rufus since the first time the quivering mess entered my vagina. But, when I wanted those toe-curling, grab the edge of the sheet moments, I reached for my well-hidden and trusty toy.

Oh, I'd gotten close several times to succumbing to temptation, the most recent time when our pool was installed. Good Lord, but the man had been a treat to watch sweat under the sun in the backyard! When Sasha casually dropped by, wearing an outfit that looked like a leftover from her hooker days, standing on a corner shaking her ample ass at potential Johns, she immediately hired *my* pool man to service her. Err, well, her pool, so she said. I'd bet my half of Carl's retirement, Sasha's "undercarriage," as she liked to refer to her lady parts, had been dirtied up numerous times by the hunky man—along with countless clients before becoming Mrs. Jermaine Rice.

Though I was excited about making Rebecca's life miserable, I was a tad nervous about spreading my legs for new meat. I'd have to make sure to buy some condoms, because the way my life was going, it would be just my luck I'd fuck Stephen, then miraculously wind up pregnant. The invasion of a new cock might wake up my dead ovaries.

Now *that* would be something! Pregnant by my sister's husband—the perfect Lifetime movie plotline!

My erotic visions of riding Stephen Wilson while he screamed, "Yeah, Roxy! Give it to me! I've wanted you forever. Rebecca is so boring compared to you! Yes, I want to feel you every day for the rest of my life! Just say the word, and I'll leave her!" disappeared when the doorbell rang, followed by several loud knocks.

Rising from the dining room table, I paused when the loud trill of an ambulance wailed in the distance. I hated the sound. It reminded me of the day Dad had a heart attack in the backyard while grilling steaks and we called 911.

Thump! Thump! Thump! "Roxy? Hurry, let me in!"

Hearing the fear in Liz's voice, I ran to the front door, wincing as a family portrait near the entryway shuddered then crashed to the floor. The glass in the frame shattered. Damn but Liz was strong. Opening the door, I asked: "What's wrong?"

Shoving me back, Liz pushed her way inside, slamming the door behind her. She looked frazzled, her appearance a mess, which *never* happened. Before she gave up her aspirations of having a real life and married old money, Liz had her heart set on becoming the next Elizabeth Arden.

The woman was so obsessed with hair and makeup she made Roger wait to take her to the hospital after her water broke just so she could fix her hair and face. Liz still adhered to the rules of suburbia.

I could tell she'd run from her house to mine, though I had no idea why. If something was so urgent, why didn't she just call?

Out of breath, Liz held up a finger. "Hang on. Let me catch my—"

"I'll get you some water."

"No. No time for that," Liz muttered, followed by a huge breath. "You need to leave. Right now."

The sirens were closer.

Shit! Did the cops find Benny's body already? I should have

taken five minutes to check the newspaper online! Maybe I was wrong and someone else was out at the cemetery yesterday and saw me bash his head in and called the police? "What? Why? Is someone hurt out there? Did one of the neighbors get hit by a car or something? Did Mrs. Goldberg have another heart attack?"

"Roxy! Listen to me. You need to leave before the press and possibly the police arrive. I dropped my cell and busted the screen, but right before that happened, I called Carol. She's on her way home. You two need to go someplace in the mountains or something."

"What in the world for?"

"Coco's dead."

The room went black, but I forced the darkness away, concentrating my gaze on the busted picture frame near the door. "Come again?"

Face flushed but breathing finally under control, Liz grabbed my arm. "Coco's dead. Elaine found her body about an hour ago, along with the words *I'm a home-wrecking whore* scrawled on her headboard in blood. Elaine freaked and called a friend at the police station, trying to keep things under wraps. I was outside trimming my roses and heard her crying, so I went to check on her. She was a mess, holding Coco's dead body against her chest, sobbing like a lost kitten. She kept saying she didn't want people to know her daughter killed herself and that she'd rather say Coco passed away from a botched abortion."

"Oh, Jesus," I moaned.

Hello, darkness. Please swallow me up now.

"At first, it looked like Coco overdosed on sleeping pills after an unsuccessful attempt to slit her wrists."

Afraid I'd pass out any second as images of me stuffing the pills down Coco's throat reappeared, I wobbled to the couch. "But, now it doesn't?"

"No! The police searched her room. I mean tore it apart just minutes ago. I was inside, sitting with Elaine, when one officer came out, holding her laptop. They found numerous saved online video chat conversations between her and Carl, including the one where Coco told him she was pregnant with his child last week. Guess he didn't realize she was recording them. One cop said that was motive, and then the coroner came out and told Elaine it was murder. Said Coco's arm was cut *after* she died, and bruising around her neck, cheeks, and arms suggested someone held her while forcing her to swallow."

"This isn't happening," I whispered, trying to keep from passing out. My blurry vision made Liz's face look like a jumbled mass of colors. My bestie's countenance was now a suburban Picasso. "Poor Elaine."

"Mr. Shock came home and started yelling, saying he was going to kill Carl. The cops had to restrain him. You know how news travels around here—it won't take long for the TV cameras to show up, and if either of the Shocks mention Carl's name, they'll head over here for an exclusive. God, I'm stunned, so I can't even imagine how you must feel. Do you think—I mean, is it even possible—Carl did this? No, no way. The evidence with Coco is gone! If he was going to try and cover up his transgressions, he'd have gone after the one still carrying his kid."

Liz kept talking, but I tuned her voice out.

Coco died *exactly* how I'd written it in my journal.

Exactly how the dream played out.

The soreness in my muscles wasn't just from the fight with Rebecca and wrangling Benny's dead weight into the grave.

I'd killed a human being last night or early this morning.

Again.

My beloved Moscato betrayed me! The yummy, fermented sweet grapes unleashed the dormant, sadistic killer inside my screwed-up head.

Fuck!

Without saying a word, I stood and raced to the kitchen, stopping short when my gaze landed on the Damascus knife block set.

The 8" chef's knife was gone.

I tried to think, make my mind engage, but it was gridlocked. Shaking, attempting to comprehend I'd crossed the line and acted out my demented fantasies, tears burst out and rolled down my cheeks.

God, my sick actions, twisted fantasies, just destroyed Carol's life.

"Roxy, why are you just standing there? You need to get going. Go, pack, and I'll wait here for Car—" Liz's words dried up as she followed my gaze. The energy level in the room spiked. "Oh, my God. Roxy?"

Turning, I looked into Liz's wide eyes. The way she stared at me, full of shock and fear, the few steps backward she took, like my murderous rampage was contagious, broke my heart. It was a foreshadowing taste of what I'd see behind Carol's eyes later.

Our lifetime of friendship, laughter, special moments, love—poof! Gone, baby. Gone.

***

Lost in a world neither of us wanted to be in, we didn't hear someone come inside the house until right behind us. "Mrs. Davenport? I'm Detective Tuck. We need to talk."

"I'll … go take care of Carol," Liz whispered.

With those words, I knew the lifelong friendship was kaput. It is one thing to be wine buddies, childhood friends, and neighbors with a crazy person, but quite another to say: "Hey, I'm best friends with a killer!"

Boy, next month's book club topic wasn't going to be about a novel. No doubt. Maybe even the entire next year.

Carol burst through the front door, those lovely green eyes I'd passed along through DNA wild with fright. "Mom? Liz? What's going on? Who the hell are you?"

Ignoring Carol's question, Detective Tuck grabbed my elbow. A slew of people dressed in blue stormed inside the house. "You'll need to come with me, please. Don't make a scene in front of your daughter, or your neighbors. Agree to come with me peaceably and I won't put you in cuffs."

A line from one of the mysteries I'd read at some point popped out of my mouth. "Not unless you're arresting me."

"If that's the way you want to play this, fine. Roxanne Davenport, you're under arrest for the murder of Coco Shock, Ginger Holloway, and Carl Davenport. You have the right to remain silent. Anything you—"

Carl? Ginger?

Well, at least he didn't include Benny Rogers.

Oh, crap. The dreams weren't dreams at all—they were memories of my drunken rampage. How many demerits does one acquire for killing their cheating husband and two of his whores in one night?

A shitload.

My fate would be sealed once the CSI team found the journal. My OCD habit about writing things down would nail me to the freaking wall.

Thanks for passing along your mental issues onto me, Mom. I said a silent prayer that the tainted DNA ended with me.

Staring at my precious child, my legs started to tremble. My little Carol. My reason for living. I'm so sorry, sweetie. I never, ever meant to hurt you. I failed the most important rule in *The Suburbia Handbook*:

Do whatever necessary, including hiding your own pain and troubles, to raise your children to be well-adjusted, productive members of society.

I didn't hear the rest of Detective Tuck's words. They were drowned out by Liz and Carol yelling.

"Are you crazy? My mom wouldn't hurt anybody! Let her go!" Carol sobbed.

"I'll call Reginald Greenwood and then Rebecca," Liz added.

A last act of kindness from my bestie?

I tried to open my mouth and say something to assure Carol and Liz everything would be okay, but nothing happened. The buzzing in my head was back, and then, my beautiful teak hardwood floor came toward me in a rush of color. The impact of my head slamming into the floor didn't even register.

Dammit. My house is dirty and I've got company. Demerit.

CHAPTER 10

Fun Q&A At The Police Station

By the time Detective Tuck pulled into the police station, three TV vans were already waiting for us.

Joy.

Once parked, he turned around and handed me a jacket. "Cover your head."

Even suburban cops are nice. Thanks, Detective.

The second the door opened, the hungry reporters shouted questions. The noise level was deafening. Tuck wrapped an arm around my back, using his own body as a shield from the throng of people. We shuffled through the masses, finally making it inside the glass doors.

Jesus, I rode in the back of a cop car and now I'm in a police station! Yet more firsts in my life. Never, even during my wild, younger days, had I been arrested or received a speeding ticket.

I'd never killed anyone, either, so there's a first for everything.

Hmm, life really does begin after forty!

Like a mute rag doll, I let the detective lead me to the booking room, never flinching when my fingerprints were taken or blinking when the mug shot was snapped. Good Lord! No makeup, hair a mess, a shiner and busted lip. My friends and neighbors would have a field day when the picture splashed across the headlines.

Thank God, my mother had no clue who I was or she'd die of a heart attack or stroke when reading or watching the news.

The entire process was over rather quickly and the detective asked me standard questions, like my full name, birthdate, social security number—none of which I answered. For some odd reason, all I could think about was Liz sitting in her gorgeous living room, tissues in hand, watching the drama of my life unfold in real time.

Court TV at its finest.

How many times over the years had we watched real-life drama on television? Good grief, way too many times to count. Like everyone else in the world, we'd been glued to the screen, spewing out our collective disgust at the awful acts of other criminals, like O. J. Simpson. The Menendez brothers. Betty Broderick. Lorena Bobbitt. Jeffrey Dahmer. Ted Bundy.

Now, Roxanne Davenport's name would be added to the list. Headlines like "Suburban Housewife Goes on Killing Spree" or "Killer Roxanne Davenport Claims Suburbia Made Her Do It" or best of all "Raging Roxy's Rampage Leaves a Trail of Death Across the 'Burbs."

Detective Tuck led me through a maze of hallways. The polished, shiny floors were slick, so I concentrated on putting one foot in front of the other. Once inside an interrogation room—holy shit, I'm in an *interrogation* room in my tattered jeans, old T-shirt, and flip flops!—I sat, grateful to be off my feet. I prayed Liz followed through and called both Rebecca and Reginald Greenwood, because I wasn't sure how long I could keep my mouth shut. I'd watched enough crime drama shows on television and knew the questions were about to come pouring out of Tuck's pursed lips. I also knew I didn't have to answer them, and just one little sentence—"I want a lawyer"—would make him stop.

Unfortunately, I was afraid of what I'd say if I opened my mouth. Instead, I kept my lips sealed.

Sitting across from me, Detective Tuck opened a thick binder. For dramatic effect, he flipped through several pages, grimacing with each flip. His friendly, dark brown eyes glanced up, staring at me. I'm sure he was making mental notes of my appearance, whether I was sweating, shaking, biting my lip, or wringing my hands.

I didn't move a muscle. I wondered which mask he'd put on first: Good cop or bad cop.

"Before we start, would you like some water? Coffee?"

Got any Moscato? I know it's early morning but I sure could use some. Oh, and a pack of smokes and a lighter. Um, make it two packs. I have a feeling I'll need them.

"No? Okay. Just let me know if you change your mind. So, Mrs. Davenport, want to tell me what happened last night?"

I didn't blink. Detective Tuck seemed to be straddling the fence—he was mediocre cop at the moment.

"Roxanne, it's okay. Just tell me your side of the story. From what information we've gathered, you've experienced some very stressful situations during the course of the last few weeks. Oh, may I call you Roxanne?"

Well, hello good cop! Nice segue from mediocracy. Call me what you like, I don't care. Your little act isn't going to work. Stressful situations? Really? That's your opening line? Pathetic. Obviously, you need to watch some episodes of *Law & Order!* Your interrogation skills suck, sir.

"Let's start by answering easy questions. How did you sustain the injuries to your face?"

Hmm, well, it's like this, Detective Fuck—er, Tuck. I have this wretched sister who screwed-up my life. You should arrest her too because she pushed me down this murderous path. Charge her as an accessory. You think I look bad? Ha! You should see *her* face.

"Come now, Roxanne. The judicial process will be easier if

you are open, honest, and forthcoming with answers. I'm giving you a chance to explain your side by telling me how you felt after finding out your husband of nearly twenty years had been unfaithful and left you for a pregnant, younger woman. How did the news make you feel when you discovered an underage neighbor had also been sleeping with him and also was carrying his child before she aborted it?"

How the fuck do you think I felt, idiot? Angry. Humiliated. Jealous. Hurt. Royally pissed off. Pick one or all! Wouldn't you be?

The friendly demeanor shifted. I could tell my lack of any response irritated Tuck. Any second, he'd jump ship and swim over to the dark side, releasing the *bad cop*.

"The coroner found traces of type AB negative blood on Coco Shock's upper torso, and according to Mrs. Shock, Coco's blood type is O positive. Your husband and Ms. Holloway were both O positive, so that rules out either of them as suspects. AB negative is the rarest blood type, only present in 1 per cent of Caucasians. What blood type are you?"

Hello, blurry vision, thanks for stopping by.

Shit.

No doubts now.

I'm AB negative.

Visions of struggling with Coco hit me. Though I was stronger and bigger, the little whore did put up a good fight. A flailing arm connected once with my lip, hard enough to make it bleed again. Damn you and your left hook, Rebecca!

"A team of forensic specialists is tearing up your house, Mrs. Davenport. They'll find evidence, like the bloody clothes and knife. It's just a matter of time."

Oh, it's Mrs. Davenport now? Uh-oh, here comes bad cop.

"Mr. Davenport had quite a few marks on his body. Older ones, not from when you killed him. Specifically, he sported some nasty cuts and bruising to his backside. We didn't find any evidence in Ms. Holloway's apartment of bondage equipment. Is that something you two enjoyed? S&M?"

Not until recently, sir. Well, at least, on my part. Apparently, Carl enjoyed being tied up and submissive. I tried the whole dominatrix thing, but just once. Long enough to bend my husband to my will! It was quite exhilarating. You should try it sometime because you look a bit uptight. How long's it been since you've taken a vacation?

Detective Tuck looked annoyed. Really annoyed. Bet he wasn't used to someone clamming up.

Just as he started to rummage through the binder, someone knocked on the door. "Excuse me."

Rising to his feet, Tuck opened the door. A young cop handed him another bulging folder, whispering the entire time. Tuck nodded. A wicked smile appeared.

Uh-oh.

They found my journal.

Did they find the clothes and empty pill bottle, too? The knife? Think, Roxy, what did you do with them? Push past the murky memories and think! Shower. Yes, I took a shower, the clothes and bottle wadded up inside several plastic grocery sacks. (Aren't those things handy for just about anything?) But, what did I do with it? I didn't see it in the bathroom earlier. Shit! I can't remember anymore.

A bucketful of demerits hovered above my head.

Closing the door, Detective Tuck lingered, perusing the contents of the folder. My stomach clenched when he removed the journal. He opened it, going to sections marked with yellow Post-It notes.

Damn.

Returning to sit across from me, he set the journal down between us. "Is this your handwriting, Mrs. Davenport?"

As a matter of fact, it is Detective Tuck. Notice the difference from one page to the next? The ones that are written in nice, loopy cursive I penned when sober. The ones that look like ramblings of a mad housewife were written when I was drunk. Alcohol turns nice penmanship into the scribblings of a child, doesn't it?

"Looks like from your entries the deceased died *exactly* how you envisioned. Isn't that interesting? Either you're clairvoyant or stupid enough to kill three people the same way you wrote it down. I don't believe in clairvoyance, Mrs. Davenport. That leaves us with you being the killer."

Ding, ding, ding! We've got a winner! Give the detective a prize. Oh, wait. You missed one—the actual number is four, not three. Awww, no prize for you.

Detective Tuck extracted several pieces of paper, pushing them toward me. Glancing down, it took a second for me to process what they were.

Statements.

"Several of your friends and neighbors told us you've exhibited odd behavior lately. Drinking too much, dressing seductively, saying hurtful, hateful things, and even becoming physically violent with your sister, Rebecca Wilson. Seems there was a nasty confrontation at her office, resulting in Mrs. Wilson suffering a broken nose. The altercation does explain your injuries, but it also shows a pattern of irrational behavior culminating with you committing multiple murders."

It sure does, sir! Wow, you're really putting the pieces of the puzzle of my fucked-up life together fast. I retract my earlier thought about you needing to watch more *Law & Order.* You're on a roll.

Shit, how much longer will it be before Reginald arrives? I'm not sure I can keep my mouth shut. It's really hot in this room. And stinky. Doesn't anyone ever clean this place? Ever heard of air freshener or scented candles, Tuck? Is the city so broke it can't afford a cleaning crew at least once a week?

Detective Tuck reached the next phase of bad cop. Red flushed his cheeks as he stood and yelled: "Mrs. Davenport! We found traces of blood on your bathroom floor and guess what? It came back as AB negative, which is the same blood type we found on Coco Shock. Your vehicle has been cleaned recently, and though it's too degraded for a sample, we did find traces of blood. A knife is missing from your kitchen—the same type and size of knife, mind you, used to stab your husband and Ginger Holloway to death inside her apartment. We've got statements of your erratic behavior from people who know you and we have the journal. Pages full of words written by you detailing the murders and also your plans to exact revenge on your sister by sleeping with her husband. Talk to me!"

You forgot the remains of my sister's boyfriend rotting in the ground at Eternal Slumber Acres, hot shot. If you've got it all figured out, Detective Tuck, why do I need to say anything? Jesus, Reginald, please get here before I snap!

"You were a busy woman last night, Mrs. Davenport. And smart. You had it all planned out and executed it perfectly, right down to changing clothes after killing Coco Shock and then heading downtown on the bus in a fresh pair. Where are both sets of clothes, Roxanne?"

First name again? Make up your mind, copper!

"Where's the knife? The empty bottle of sleeping pills we know you had a prescription for? Cooperate with me, Roxanne. Come clean and tell me your side of the story while I'm still interested in hearing it. If you do, I'll ask the prosecuting attorney to not seek the death penalty."

Death penalty? Oh, now there's a phrase I never thought I'd hear someone say to *and* about me! Wow, I didn't even know our state still had that rule on the books! Didn't that barbaric practice end centuries ago? Good heavens, I'm letting this smarmy detective get to me. That was a good scare tactic but it won't matter because I honestly can't answer your questions, Detective Dickhead, because I don't remember.

To bring his point home and attempt to break my will, Tuck

pulled out a photo from the folder. He slammed it down in front of me.

Sure enough, there it was, plain as day in the image. Though a bit grainy, the picture was clear. There I was, getting on the bus dressed in black leggings, black hooded sweatshirt, sunglasses covering my eyes.

Oh, shit. I broke. "Lawyer. Right now."

"Fuck!" Detective Tuck yelled while slamming his fist into the wall. Without giving me another glance, he stormed out of the room. Seconds ticked by, my gaze was locked onto the picture, the infernal buzzing inside my mind back.

There it was, right in front of me—the undeniable proof of last night's activities.

The door opened and Reginald Greenwood walked in. Dressed to perfection, looking every part the shyster lawyer; I felt my breath leave my lungs. The shakes set in.

"Please tell me you didn't say anything," Reginald whispered after sitting down across from me. He opened his briefcase, extracting a yellow legal pad.

"No, I didn't, except to ask for you," I choked out in a raspy whisper.

"Thank God!"

"Please tell me you smoke? I'm dying for one."

Reginald shook his head. "You're in a world of trouble, Roxanne. A world of trouble"

"I'm in more than you know, Reginald."

Reginald's thick eyebrows raised in confusion. "Explain that statement. Right now."

You really should consider taking a different tone with me, counselor. I've just been charged with not one, or two, but *three* counts of premeditated murder. Show some freaking fear! Instead, I took a cleansing breath and said: "I did it, Reginald. I don't want to go through the nightmare of a trial. The thought of all my family's dirty laundry bared in open court for all to see and hear makes me ill. I lost it after my sister died and then everything else. I couldn't take the pressure of watching my once-blissful life come apart at the seams. Plead me out, Reginald. Don't try to bargain with them about my sentence. I'll take whatever they offer."

Reginald's mouth dropped open. "Roxanne, that's crazy!"

"So am I, Reginald, and I certainly don't need a shrink to peek inside my head to confirm it. Crazy as a loon, but it's what I want. What I deserve. Do it."

"Not until you tell me why."

"I just did, Reginald. Didn't you hear me?"

"Yes, but that's not the only reason. I can see it all over your face. Why this route, Roxy?"

Crossing my arms, the defiant Roxy rose to the occasion. "Make the deal first. Get me in front of the judge, let me take the punishment and the case be over. Then, I'll tell you all the juicy details. Oh, and one more thing."

"What?"

"I haven't used my one phone call yet. Is it still available to me?"

"Well, yes, but the call is usually reserved for contacting a lawyer."

"I need about five minutes and privacy. Can you arrange that? Maybe tell them I want to speak with another attorney or something?"

"I'll try, but can't promise you privacy. Who are you calling?"

"That's none of your concern, Reginald. Just make it happen."

Rubbing his forehead, Reginald shook his head. "Clients like you make me question my career choice. You realize this might take a while, which means you'll be stuck here, right?"

"Right. I couldn't afford to bond out anyway. Just get it done, Reginald. Fast. I'm not putting my daughter through any more than I already have."

"Fine, but for the record, I disagree with your decision. Heartily disagree."

"Yeah, well, I don't care. It's my life; my choice. Go. I need to make that phone call."

Reginald sighed and left, slamming the door behind him. In a few minutes, he came back, handing me his cell. "You've got five minutes. Don't make me regret sticking my neck out for you by hiring another lawyer and using my phone to do it."

"I won't," I muttered.

***

I waited for Reginald to leave the room then dialed. The conversation wasn't pleasant, but thankfully, lasted less than the allotted five minutes. Satisfied, I hung up and set the phone down.

***

Reginald returned, snatched it off the table, and left without another word.

***

A female cop arrived a few minutes later. She put me in handcuffs—not the soft, fuzzy ones like I used on Carl—and led me to a holding cell.

I didn't cry, or shake, or come apart at the seams. Nope. Instead, I stared at the ugly gray concrete, fully aware, perhaps for the first time in my life, what I was doing.

And why.

Suburbia Handbook Rule Number Eleven: One must defend their family, no matter what. This rule trumps everything else.

Period.

After all the attempts to steer clear of my old life, I was still a housewife at heart.

CHAPTER 11

Jailhouse Visit

"You've got a visitor."

"Is it my lawyer?"

"I'm not your appointment secretary. Get up."

Crossing my arms, I remained seated on the small bunk. Wow, did I miss my king-sized bed and clean sheets. Oh, and the fresh scent of my favorite laundry detergent. My cleaning obsession remained in constant overdrive in jail and there wasn't a thing I could do about it. "Not unless you tell me who it is. I've made it very clear I won't talk to any reporters. Don't visitors have to sign a log or something?"

The gruff female guard glared at me through the bars. The woman was in serious need of a makeover, including a thorough waxing of her overgrown eyebrows and chin hair. Every time she passed by my cell, I wanted to yell: "Hey, you realize we're supposed to have two separate brows, and chin hair only belongs on pigs, right?"

"Female. Said she's a relative. Move, now."

My heart skipped two beats. The thought of seeing Carol made me feel light-headed. I'd given strict instructions to Reginald regarding my daughter. She was not to set foot inside the jail. Maybe it was Liz? Oh, please, cosmos. Let it be my bestie. I'm dying to see a face that looks normal. "Again, I'm not going anywhere until you know for sure. Reporters have been known to lie for an exclusive."

Anger flickered in the guard's ugly eyes. Leaning closer to the bars, she whispered: "And older, rich bitches like you have been known to kill people when they don't get their way. Boo-hoo. You couldn't stand the thought of lifting a dainty finger and working after your husband left you high and dry for some younger pussy. I'm swooning with sympathy for you over here. Get up, right now, or I just might accidentally move you out of this solitary cell and into gen pop."

Okay, you repellant hag. You've got me there. I need to keep my cool and play along. If it is some reporter, I'll simply clamp my mouth shut like I did with ol' Detective Tuck.

Sticking my wrists through the appointed slot, I let the woman cuff me without saying another peep.

After traversing numerous hallways, she stopped at a small room and pointed. "Ten minutes is all you've got. Talk fast."

Fuck you, Unibrow. Why don't you use the time to find a mirror and do something about your unruly facial hair? Perhaps make an appointment with your gynecologist to discuss your hormonal balance issues?

Once the hag opened the door and I saw who was on the other side of the glass, a phone receiver held up against her ear (with a Wet Wipe, of course) I gasped.

Rebecca looked awful. A huge bandage covered her nose, both eyes rimmed in black and blue. It was the first time I'd seen her without full makeup since she'd hit puberty. Yeah, I did that, and the damage to her face was the one thing I accomplished in recent weeks with no regrets.

If my uptight, twatwaffle sister came for a visit, something was wrong. A sense of fear ambled up my spine. Once seated in the uncomfortable chair, I lifted the receiver. "Is Carol okay?"

"She's fine, Roxy, considering things."

"Then why are you here? Did some reporter dangle money in front of you for a jailhouse exclusive? Are you wired?"

Rebecca snorted then grimaced. "I've got plenty of money, so, no. Have I been approached by some? Oh, yes. I had to change my cell and home numbers this week, and I've been working from home since the day after all this mess started. They're relentless. You're famous, er, rather, infamous."

God, I wished the plexiglass separating us would disappear, just for a minute. Long enough for me to yank out the new extensions from her head and shove them down her throat. Oh, better yet! Wrap them around her neck and squeeze until she quit breathing. Death by hair! "So, you came to gloat?"

A few tears appeared and a hint of sadness flashed behind her swollen eyes. It was the first time since Rachel's funeral she'd displayed real, true emotions. "You really think I'm that kind of person, Roxanne?"

I suppressed a laugh. L.B. hadn't addressed me as Roxanne since, well, ever. The way she said it was akin to the motherly tone I'd use when angry at Carol. The haughtiness in her voice—the superior attitude—made me wish I'd ignored my broken twat the day of our battle in her office and finished what I started. "I don't think—I know. Any previous doubts I had disappeared my first day at work, or don't you remember?"

"Yes, I do," Rebecca whispered, a few tears escaping and sliding down her cheeks. "For that, for all this, what it all led to, I'm sorry. Seeing up close and personal how all of this has affected Carol—it's broken me. Knocked down the walls I built years ago. Made me actually feel pity and remorse for my actions, believe it or not. That's why I'm here—to apologize."

My God.

All the levels of Hell just froze over as pigs flew by on rainbow-colored unicorns dropping fragrant, glittery farts from the sky.

Rebecca Denise Rayburn Wilson just said words I doubt she'd ever spoken to anyone. Scrutinizing her face, I searched for any signs of deceit or trickery. Seeing none, realizing she was serious, made a lump form in my throat.

"Actions speak louder than words, Rebecca. Show me by taking care of Carol and Mom. They're all that matter to me."

"Me, too." Rebecca wiped away the droplets on her chin. "And I will, just like I promised. We've made sure to keep the press and others away, to give Carol a chance to deal with this mess without being bombarded by questions or bright lights and cameras shoved into her face. The only thing we couldn't stop was the police interrogation. The good news is they didn't ask her much. It was all about you and what you've been up to and only lasted about forty minutes."

"We?"

"Liz took her to a cabin up north as soon as the interrogation was over. Stephen and I rearranged our work schedules today. We leave tomorrow so Liz can come back."

Choking back tears, I nodded. I'd give up my life to hold my daughter, stroke her hair, coo gentle reassurances into her ear that everything will be all right, just like I did when she was little. Just one more time, one more chance to shelter my child from the raging storms of life. "Thank you, Rebecca. Please make sure to tell Liz and Stephen I appreciate everything they're doing for my daughter."

"I will. We're rallying behind her, so don't worry. You've got enough on your plate. Have you been able to watch or read any news?"

"No. Even if I could, I wouldn't. I have zero interest in seeing or reading what sort of spin is put on all this. Why?"

"Snippets of your journal were leaked yesterday."

Shit. I bet Sasha would read it out loud at next book club. Denise and the rest of the repellant hags will drool like Pavlov dogs, hanging on every word, and then grouse and gush for freaking *years.* "Not surprising. I'm sure someone pocketed a good chunk of cash to leak it. I bet it was Detective Tuck. He was really pissed when I didn't answer any of his questions."

Swallowing hard, Rebecca returned the scrutinizing gaze. "Were you really going to do it? Sleep with Stephen just to get back at me? Have a party with all our friends and humiliate me by showing you two screwing?"

"Yes," I sighed, deciding to come clean since it was out in the open. "I was quite angry after what you did to me. To Carol."

Awkward silence.

We stared at each other through plastic as though really seeing the other person across from them for the first time.

"Guess I had it coming after what I did, for what I started. I only wanted to hurt you, not Carol. Anger gave me tunnel vision."

"Yeah, it works that way, which is why I'm on this side of the glass."

More awkward silence.

Rebecca looked like she was about to toss her lunch all over the plexiglass.

"I moved Mom to another facility under a false name. She's not doing well. Even with her memory gone, it's like something inside her knows the truth. She's not eating and refuses to take her meds. Dr. Kilgore said he thinks she's willing herself to die. I thought you needed to know."

Oh, Mom. I'm so sorry. "God, did some—?"

"Yes, two reporters managed to slip inside at the old facility," Rebecca interrupted. "They probably paid off a nurse or something. Mom's dementia turned out to be a blessing. I walked in right when one reporter plopped a newspaper in front of her with your mug shot. She had no clue it was you."

"Bastards. Thanks for stepping up to the plate, Rebecca. Not just for Mom, but for Carol."

A hint of anger flared in Rebecca's eyes. "You really didn't leave me much choice, Roxy. Your actions put me in this position."

“Ditto,” I replied with a cold, harsh tone.

The word hung heavy between us. We both knew there wasn’t anything else left to say that hadn’t already been spoken.

Biting her lip, Rebecca replaced the receiver and stood, never giving me a second glance as she left the room.

I did the same.

CHAPTER 12

Hot Headlines – Suburbia Made Her Do It!

The next few weeks were a blur. When not crammed inside the small cell, listening to the conversations of other female inmates, smelling horrid odors or dreading using the nasty toilet, I did get to go outside for an hour. Dressed in an awful shade of orange, feet clad in hard, plastic shower shoes, a high chain-link fence surrounded with scary-looking razor wire, I absorbed as much vitamin D as possible.

To keep my mind and body occupied while caged like an animal, I paced back and forth, did sit-ups, push-ups, and squats. Though I hated being locked up, the vigorous workouts toned my body. At least I'd look good in front of the court. If cameras were allowed inside, my former friends couldn't give me a demerit for looking rough!

Score!

Most of the female jailers were bitches, but two of them were sort of nice. One in particular, Juanita Sanchez, grinned at me every time she passed by, a knowing look on her face. She'd even slipped me some chocolate and smokes, which were both appreciated. Now, if I could just convince her to get me some Moscato …

Footsteps approached. I hoped the person coming down the hall was Juanita. Today was my big day in front of Judge Clemmons—the allocution hearing. According to Reginald, I'd get the chance to really clean up, put some makeup on and fix my dull, lifeless hair, before court.

"Hey, Roxy. You ready?"

Thank goodness it was Juanita. In her hands, she held my best outfit. I wondered if Liz or Carol brought it? There was no way it'd been L.B.

"Ready as I'll ever be, Juanita."

Unlocking the cell, Juanita motioned for me to come out. "You remember the way to the showers, right?"

"Yep," I replied, leading the way. I was beyond thankful Juanita hadn't shackled my hands and feet. Those things hurt! Bondage aficionados were strange people, for sure.

Once in the bathroom, which resembled the one I remembered from high school, I let out a sigh of relief. Privacy! Finally! Showering in front of others wasn't something I enjoyed.

"You get an extra five minutes today, Roxy. I brought you some scented soap too. Hope you like Morning Rain."

"Considering the nasty soap I've been using, it will be like a trip to the spa, I'm sure. You guys must have an account with Granny Clampett or something."

"Huh?"

"*The Beverly Hillbillies*? Granny Clampett? She made lye soap in a big black kettle out by the cement pond."

"Is that a TV show or something?"

Shaking my head, I stripped and stuck my hand out for the toiletries. "Yes. You can catch the reruns on late-night TV. Funny show."

Looking at her watch, Juanita grimaced. "You need to hurry, Roxy."

"Okay."

The plastic bag Juanita handed me was full of hotel-sized

shampoo, conditioner, and the fresh-smelling soap. For the first time in weeks, I felt like a normal person.

Once finished and dried, Juanita led me to a side room I'd never been in before. A placard above the door read "Women's Preparation Room," and I almost laughed.

Nothing inside that room could prepare me for what I was about to do in front of a packed courtroom.

Nothing.

"Here," Juanita whispered once we were inside. "When your sister brought your clothes, she also left some makeup. I'll have to throw away what you don't use, and please don't tell anyone I gave it to you. I'd get into a lot of trouble."

Smiling, I sat down in front of a dirty mirror, shocked L.B. had allowed herself to stoop to the level of delivery girl. "I won't, Juanita. Thank you for this and for being so nice to me. I do appreciate it. I hope some of the guards at the prison are as nice as you."

Juanita scowled, her pretty dark brown eyes reflecting a bit of sadness. "They won't be, Roxy. Those bitches are mean and nothing more than men trapped inside women's bodies. You'll need to watch yourself, and I don't mean just from the other inmates."

Dabbing at my face, I began the process of putting makeup on. At least the scar on my lip wasn't red anymore and the shiners were gone.

"Don't you think my reputation will follow and scare off potential problems?"

"Doubtful. Whoever gets to you will score points. It always works that way when a highprofile inmate arrives."

"Just like TV, huh?" I muttered.

"Yeah, just like it."

As I swooped on mascara—thanks, Rebecca, for bringing me Lancôme—I'm surprised it isn't generic shit, I noticed Juanita seemed antsy. "What's on your mind, Juanita?"

Glancing around to ensure we were still alone, Juanita sat down next to me. In a low whisper, she asked: "Did you really do it? Kill three people?"

"I did." The itch to say four danced on the tip of my tongue, yet I held it in.

Juanita grinned. "I don't blame you one bit. If my husband ever did anything like that to me, I'd consider doing the same thing! Lots of women would, or at least, they'd want to. I'm not saying killing them was the right choice, but in your case, it's understandable."

"No, it wasn't right, Juanita. If I could go back in time, I wouldn't make the same choices. My actions hurt too many people. I snapped in a moment of weakness, and now, I have to live with the consequences."

"Yes, but you've handled things with such class! Most women would make sure to take the stand, tell the world what a horrible person their spouse was, how he'd hurt them and broke them down. Plead their case in front of the court of public opinion! Beg for understanding and mercy. Not you! You did it, admitted to it, and didn't let your life become a freak circus in front of the court or the masses. That takes guts and tremendous strength. You've got a lot of fans in your corner who think you're great, Roxy. A lot."

Grimacing, I rose from the bench and started dressing. "They shouldn't. What I did was wrong. And just like my daddy raised me to do, I'll take what's owed to me. What's the old saying? 'Don't do the crime if you can't do the time'?"

"Yes, that's the one."

"I don't want to do the time, Juanita. I don't. I threw away my entire life, ended the lives of three others because I'm weak, not strong. Think about all I've lost and what I took from others. When you do, I guarantee you'll no longer be a fan."

I noticed tears fill Juanita's pretty eyes before she brushed them away. Nodding once, she didn't say anything else.

Dressed and shoes on, I took one last look in the mirror. It would be the final time I looked like the old Roxy, just with a scar on my lip and about ten pounds of new muscle. To my surprise, I felt a lump form in my throat.

"Come on, it's time," Juanita urged. "I'm sorry, but you'll need to wear these in court."

Holding out my wrists, I let Juanita cuff me. Memories of the night I'd tortured Carl burst forth, but they were sort of fuzzy, like watching an old TV show, and disappeared quickly.

My shoes made a strange sound on the concrete as we walked through the halls. I was glad the courtroom and jail were attached so I didn't have to go outside and be accosted by reporters. Enough of them would be in the courtroom, and at least inside, they couldn't ask me questions or take pictures.

Juanita stopped at the door leading inside. "I'll walk you to the table with your attorney and then remove the cuffs. Ready?"

Taking a deep breath, I closed my eyes. "Ready."

The second the door opened, I was bombarded with stimulation. The courtroom was packed, eager faces staring at me while watching me walk across the floor. Reginald, dressed in a black suit with a red tie, looked dapper and serene. My throat locked up when I noticed Liz, Rebecca, and Carol in the first bench directly behind him.

Oh dear Jesus.

My lovely daughter looked awful.

Dark circles rimmed Carol's eyes, tears spilling down pale, gaunt cheeks as I passed by. The sounds of murmured voices rose. A wave of dizziness threatened to overtake me, but I pushed on, determined to do what I came here for before passing out.

Now that would be a headline!

Juanita removed the cuffs and walked over to stand by the side door. The smell of Reginald's expensive cologne made me sad because it was the same scent Carl wore.

Leaning over, Reginald whispered: "You're sure this is what

you want? The second Judge Clemmons takes the bench it'll be too late. I can always change the plea to not guilty by reason of mental disease or defect, because God knows you're certifiable."

"I'm sure, Reginald. Trust me. And remember, once the case is over, we'll need to talk. I do get to have private visits with my attorney in prison, correct?"

"Yes."

"Good. Then let's do this."

"All rise for the Honorable Harold Clemmons."

Here we go, Roxy. I mentally hummed "It's the End of the World," by R.E.M., changing the lyrics to "It's the end of the world as I've known it, and I don't feel fine."

***

The nightmare was over in less than half an hour. As part of the plea deal taking the death penalty off the table, I answered the judge's questions, admitted to all three murders, asked for mercy for my wayward ways, and poof! I was sentenced to life in prison.

That certainly wasn't part of the rulebook or my life plan. Demerit!

Sobs from behind me made tears of my own escape. Carol wailed: "No, Mom. No! What you did—it's not right!"

Looking at Reginald, he nodded once. Turning, I stepped over to the railing, reaching out for my daughter. Carol buried her face in my chest. The imprinted smell of my child, feeling her thin body quake in my arms, experiencing every bit of her pain and sorrow, I wept. "I love you, Carol Claire. You've always been my reason for living."

"Mom, why? Why did you do it?" Carol sobbed. "It was so wrong!"

Juanita was back. I felt her fingers around my elbow. "I'm sorry, Mrs. Davenport, but it's time to go."

Rebecca and Liz both stood, each taking one of Carol's arms, prying her body from mine. Unable to stand, Carol collapsed into Liz's waiting arms. Through the blur of my tears, I locked gazes with Rebecca and mouthed, "Promise me?"

With tears cascading down her cheeks over the big bandage covering a broken nose, Rebecca nodded and whispered: "Promise."

Well, well, well. The Grinch really did grow a heart.

I'll be damned.

All it took to do so was watching her older sister go to prison.

The song "Cold Hearted Snake," by Paula Abdul seemed appropriate, so I hummed it inside my head as Juanita led me out of the courtroom. If I still had a cell phone, that's the song I'd assign to Rebecca. She'd lost the moniker of Lunatic Bitch.

I owned the title now.

CHAPTER 13

Coming Clean

The second week of my incarceration—oh, just saying the word is a demerit—I finally had a visit from Reginald. True to my word, I told him everything from beginning to end, except for the little rotting secret at Eternal Slumber Acres. By the time I finished the sordid tale and explained the rules he was to follow, he looked like he was about to throw up. The news aged him in seconds. I wondered how long it would be before he made an appointment with his doctor for another injection of Botox to erase all his new worry lines. Minutes? Hours? Days?

Nope, not days. Reginald M. Greenwood, Esquire, probably had his plastic surgeon on speed dial and would call from the parking lot since he certainly wasn't a stranger to using chemicals to look younger. Judging by the tightness around his eyes and neck, he'd gone under the knife at least once, too.

"You make sure my sister adheres to the rules, Reginald. I mean it."

Shaking his head, Reginald stood, pacing back and forth in small circles on the ugly, mint green floor. The tiles looked like they'd been in place since the dawn of time. They were stained, cracked, and so out of style. Mint green. Seriously? Who picks that as a color palette choice?

"Crazy. No doubt about it. Life in suburbia fried your brain. Trying to keep up with the Joneses cracked you like a fragile egg."

"Reginald, you gave me your word. I would hate to have to tell the world you knew about all of this and agreed to help me."

Reginald's gaze could have melted steel. "And I don't intend on going back on it, even if I wanted to because the attorney/client rules still apply. Damn! I could lose my license, and there's a slim chance I could be charged with all sorts of things from to fraud to aiding and abetting and even facilitating murder. If just one piece of this comes out, the questions will begin, asking me how much I knew before your allocution hearing. Jesus, Roxanne. You've really put me in a bad spot."

"Trade places with me then you'll understand what being in a bad spot is all about. Trust me."

"I'm having a difficult time grasping all this."

"Welcome to my world."

A stain of red spread up from Reginald's neck to his face as the enormity of what I shared hit him. "Let me see if I got all this right. You killed Coco."

"Yes." Ding dong the little bitch is dead!

"Snuck out of your house, half-drunk, in the middle of the night, got her to let you into her bedroom window under the false pretense something was wrong with Carl, then killed her by forcing her to ingest your sleeping pills."

"You're on the straight and narrow road, Reginald."

Glaring at me, Reginald snapped. "This isn't funny, Roxanne! Not in the slightest."

Careful, counselor. Those worry lines are like rabbits fucking in the woods—they multiply at a phenomenal rate when under stress. "Sorry. Guess I inherited my father's twisted sense of humor."

"You came back home and disposed of your clothes, though you don't recall where. And the police never found them."

Reginald wasn't asking questions at this point. He was just rehashing what I'd said, so I didn't respond. I'd let him run with it.

"But you didn't kill Carl or Ginger?"

I shook my head.

"Jesus, no wonder no forensic evidence tying you there was ever found! None at all. No hair, fiber, fingerprints. Cash used on the bus; the sunglasses. Just like you wrote it down, except you didn't do it."

God, I wish I had. I really did. Though I didn't enjoy the label of killer, I preferred it only hovered over my head rather than another's as well. "No."

"Because your drunken ass came home after killing a 16-year-old neighbor girl, wobbled upstairs, took a shower, stuffed your clothes and the empty pill bottle in a sack and then passed out on the bathroom floor! And you left your fucking journal on the table downstairs—detailing every single crime. My God, Roxanne! What were you thinking?"

"I wasn't, Reginald. I was drunk, angry, and really, really pissed off at a lot of people! Try putting yourself in my shoes just for a minute. Every hit I took during that month ate away at my sanity. Drinking didn't help the situation, either. There might be other issues as well that helped cause this, but none of that matters now."

Spinning around, Reginald's face drained of all color. "What does that mean? There's more?"

Oops, I almost made a significant slip! Reginald would have a heart attack if I spilled the news about Benny's rotting corpse, and the diagnosis from Dr. Critchon. "It just means I snapped, Reginald. Rebecca's little game was the last straw. I tried to hold it together, but I lost the battle. Do I regret killing Coco? Part of me does, yet part of me wants to give myself a high five for taking the tramp out before she ruined someone else's life. Sick, huh? The worst part about this whole nightmare is not the murders. It's who did them and why."

"You didn't realize what really happened until Detective Tuck showed you the photo from the bus, did you?"

"No! Everything was so jumbled inside my mind that morning. Can you blame me? I'd been betrayed by my wretched sister, got into a freaking fight with her the day before and then woken up from a horrible dream. A dream that played out in reality the way I wrote it, so, of course, when I heard about Coco's death, then Carl's, and Ginger's, I immediately concluded the dreams were memories. I lost it after I saw the picture. Everything became clear then and I knew what I had to do."

"To save Carol," Reginald responded, rubbing his damp forehead.

"Yes, to save my daughter. It's one thing to wake up and discover you've killed, Reginald. Quite another to realize your daughter did, too. I couldn't handle the guilt and shame. It's my fucking fault!"

"What did she do with both sets of clothes, Roxanne? The knife? The pill bottle? We need to know and make sure they're never found."

"They're long gone, Reginald. Don't worry. My daughter's no fool. She made sure of it."

"You're putting your life—and my reputation—in the hands of the girl who killed her father and a woman pregnant with her half-sister in cold blood! Oh, and one, mind you, who left the journal out in plain view—"

"Best not to let your emotions get the upper hand, counselor. Look what happened to me when I did."

Gritting his teeth, Reginald huffed: "Location, Roxanne! This is critical! The knife and clothing are the only pieces of evidence tying Carol to the murders!"

"Fine, worrywart. She took everything and tossed them into

the dumpster at work. The trash was emptied that morning. I sure do wish she'd have included my journal, but wishes don't always come true, right?"

"How can you be so cavalier about this? I mean, how do you know for sure Carol got rid of the items? I thought your only visitor when in jail was your sister? Did Carol tell you?"

"That's who I called from your phone: My sister. I figured Carol had already told her the truth, and I was right. I told Rebecca she's the one who started this mess and it was time for her to step up and help Carol. I admitted to killing Coco. Rebecca shared the happy news about her niece using the instructions from my drunken ramblings as a guide to kill Carl and Ginger. That broke ol' L.B.'s spirit. Other than our baby sister Rachel, Rebecca only truly loves another person, and that's my daughter."

"L.B.?"

"Oh, sorry. Nickname. Means lunatic bitch."

Reginald snorted. "Of course it does. Your entire family is nuts. I should have gone with my gut instinct and forced you to plead not guilty by reason of insanity, because you're certifiable. You don't belong in here—you belong in a straightjacket."

"Watch it, counselor. It was a man who drove me to that point. A man who suffered terrible bouts of blue-brain stupidity that culminated in his death. Carl wasn't the first and he certainly won't be the last Neanderthal controlled by an engorged penis."

"Touché, Roxanne," Reginald answered. Stopping by the window, he looked through the bars for a few seconds with a strange, haunted look on his face. "You took the fall for your daughter. As a father, I understand the desire. I wouldn't do it, mind you, but I understand. So now, you want me to make sure Rebecca follows through with her promises. Ensure Carol attends therapy sessions, finishes college, and to handle all the legal aspects of the house, vehicles, and your mother's home?"

"Correct. You aren't in charge because that's all Rebecca's punishment for starting this mess. She gets to step up to the plate and act like a loving, caring aunt and daughter. You're simply providing backup, legal, supervisory backup. You'll be the voice inside Rebecca's mind, pushing her to do the right thing by her niece and mother."

"How do you know Carol will agree to all of this? What if her mental state is too far gone and she kills again?"

"She won't, Reginald. Just like I won't. We weren't closet homicidal maniacs, for Godsakes. Okay, maybe I was after years upon years of wearing the fake mask of a serene, suburban housewife. Carol is still young, so there's time to undo the damage. We are simply two women pushed over the edge by circumstances out of our control. We've always been close, except for the horrible puberty years. My daughter mimicked my actions, much to my dismay. I won't let her do it again."

"This is so wrong, Roxanne. Carol needs—"

Okay, legal beagle. You just overstepped your bounds. No one tells me what my daughter needs. No one. "The discussion is over. You need my daughter to overcome this tragedy almost as much as I do if you want your precious reputation to be spared. Do it, Reginald. Help my daughter walk down a new path, become the woman she was meant to be, not a duplicated copy of me. Please?"

"Fine," Reginald muttered. "But I'm not doing this because I want to. You've given me no choice here so I have to. I hope you're right about your daughter, Roxanne. I really hope you're right."

"I know I am, Reginald. I didn't raise her to be a suburban housewife. I raised her to be a strong, independent woman; a doormat to no one. Like the headlines said, living in suburbia drove me to madness. My daughter has a chance to live the life she should lead, not one shifted in another direction because of one misstep."

"I don't consider killing two people a misstep and neither does the law. The crime scene was horrific. Bloody. That girl unleashed a lot of anger and fury, up close and personal."

"In her case, it was. She'll follow a new road, travel the right path. I know it. I wouldn't have bet the rest of my life on it if I had any doubts."

Grabbing his briefcase from the table, Reginald scowled. "Don't forget you risked mine and the rest of my family's, too, Roxanne. Looks like my punishment is getting to spend the rest of my life praying you made the right decision."

"Ditto. Oh, one more thing?"

"What?"

"Make sure to tell Rebecca not to let Carol come visit me until she's ready. I want her to concentrate on healing and her schoolwork, not dealing with the fact she has to visit her mother behind bars. Okay?"

"Fine." Reginald gave me one last dirty look then left me standing in the attorney/inmate visiting room.

I watched him walk away while doing the same thing he said he'd do: Praying I made the right choice.

CHAPTER 14

Orange Is Not A Good Color On Anyone

For the next three months, I learned to acclimatize to my new surroundings. Living in an eight-by-eight cell on an uncomfortable mattress in desperate need of being burned was such fun. Not! Febreze, people! Buy some! Better yet, have you heard about a nifty new product called bleach? It works great on all those stains from God-only-knows-what type of bodily fluids left behind by the previous occupants of this hellhole. Seriously—hit up the dollar store and fill up the cart! Prison is freaking demerit central!

Every single minute of my life was controlled by someone else. Freedom and privacy were no longer in my vocabulary. Ding! Time for breakfast. Ding! Time for lunch. Ding! Outside to exercise. Ding! Off to my new job, which pays nothing—sort of like being a wife. That part I was used to and it didn't bother me so much. Ding! Time for dinner. Ding! Bed check.

The food was beyond wretched. Perhaps the prison used Beef Medley dog chow to stretch the food budget? It wouldn't surprise me in the least because it was so disgusting it made school cafeteria slop seem like five-star meals and lunch ladies across the nation Top Chefs.

I missed Moscato and smoking whenever I wished.

Using the bathroom in private.

Laughing with Liz.

The painful visits with Mom.

Book club.

My house.

Carl, or at least, the younger version I like to remember, the sexy football player who made my knees weak.

Hell, a small part of me even missed Rebecca.

Oh, that's it! I really am crazy if I miss Lunatic Bitch!

All those things combined didn't even add up to the pain of missing Carol. Every night I sobbed quietly inside my dark cell, wishing I could change the way things happened.

But, I couldn't. Carol's life was ruined by a pathetic father and a sick, warped mother.

At night, I thought back over every detail of the month our lives changed, and concluded when Carol went to eat with Carl he must have spilled the beans. The scumbag told our naïve, unprepared 18-year-old the real reasons behind our divorce and the news about soon becoming an older sister. The conversation must have broken Carol's heart, and she raced home to talk to me, only to find me passed out on the floor of the bathroom, clothes, bloody knife, and an empty pill bottle inside a bag.

And then, she found my journal.

Perhaps it was the other way around and Carol found the journal first. She came home to a dark house, assumed I was asleep, decided to snoop and see what I'd been writing. In the end, the order didn't matter. What mattered was Carol's young mind snapped, just like my older one had, and the sick, sadistic plans I'd written down gave her the idea to unleash her pain.

When Liz appeared at the front door and dropped the bomb about Coco's murder, I was so stunned I didn't grasp the news about Carl's and Ginger's deaths. Not even when being interrogated at the police station. It wasn't until I saw the photo of a woman who looked just like me standing on the steps of a bus, did I realize I didn't know where Ginger Holloway lived—which meant I didn't kill my husband or Hottie Habanero.

The woman in black on the bus did.

The woman wearing Carol's sunglasses.

Carol.

My clone. A girl with jet-black hair, long legs, ample chest.

Part of me died right there in the police station while staring at the image of my little girl on her way to kill her father and his whore.

Demerit overload! Danger, Will Robinson! Danger!

The first two months of my time behind bars I was a basket case, barely sleeping, reliving all the things I'd done wrong, culminating in the utter destruction of Carol's life. When my mind wandered back to high school and college, a twinge of remorse for beating Carl's ass surfaced. It didn't last long and, honestly, all of the happy memories of our life together didn't seem to be enough for me to shed one tear over what happened to him.

Not even one little whimper.

How fucked-up is that? I'd spent half my life beside the man and bore his child, sharing intimate moments both physically and sexually, yet no tears? Did I lose my moral compass somewhere along the journey to adulthood?

Did I ever even have one?

Yes, I did but it shattered the day at the cemetery.

The only good thing to come out of this was most of the other inmates steered clear of me. Not just because I'm a tall, strong woman, or they feared me, though I think a few did. Most seemed to stand back and sort of look at me with a weird sense of awe, all fully aware who, and why, I murdered.

Liz and Juanita were right on that part—other women who'd been cheated on would gravitate to my life story, and they did. Reporters still tried to see me, though I refused to meet with even one. Piles of mail arrived for me each week from fans, which

I tossed, along with several offers from publishers about writing a book.

Pathetic. I'm a cold-bloodied killer yet some seemed to revere me as a quasi-celebrity. What is wrong with people? What happened to revering real heroes, like our soldiers, first responders, or even comic book characters? When did humanity's collective mindset shift and start revering monsters? Suburbia—no, the entire world—needs an enema.

Stat.

The third month, probably because I'd been a "housewife" in my former life, I was assigned to work in the kitchen. There weren't a whole lot of ingredients to work with and I was thrilled I never spotted one can of dog food hidden on the back shelves. But I did alter some of the dishes, adding different spices and such, making the food easier to eat.

Though I didn't enjoy my new digs or the thought of spending the rest of my life incarcerated, what bothered me the most were the pockets of confusion and missing chunks of time I'd lost. True to my previous nature, I kept a journal, detailing my thoughts and experiences behind bars. I'd write things down, read them once and then crush the sheets of paper into tight balls, flushing them down the commode. I feared one day I'd write something I shouldn't and the wrong person would get their hands on it and ruin Carol's life.

Again.

That just *wouldn't* do at all. Yes, I attempted to live my life by a new set of rules, but one from the old *Handbook* was permanently entrenched inside my heart.

Rule Number Eleven: One must defend their family, no matter what. The rule trumps everything else, even if the defense comes in the form of bodily harm to another or the destruction of the defender.

Oh look! A credit in my jar—one no one would ever see since it was overshadowed by demerits.

It took a lot of effort to toss out my words, since I'd been such an obsessed note taker my entire life. All my thoughts, worries, fears, dreams for Carol; the words were sections of my soul and it somehow felt wrong to throw pieces of myself down the can. I cried the first time I watched the paper disappear down the drain.

I mean, seriously, I need *something* to do besides stare at the gray walls and flooring, counting bugs. Sometimes, I'd be in the middle of a sentence and stop, my mind completely blank as to what I'd been thinking, or able to recall what my day had been like.

These issues started last year but only happened sporadically. I'd attributed them to bouts with too much alcohol and, like Carl said, the stress of losing my father, Mom's downward slide into dementia, and Rachel's death. After the terrible phone call from Dr. Critchon, being sober for over three months, the rate which the memory lapses and confusion increased, I knew better. I'd seen it all before from the outside and now from the inside. The knowledge terrified me.

Sometimes, when the bell rang in the morning, I'd wake up in a complete state of panic, no clue where I was, and start screaming. Then, last Tuesday, during the twice-weekly mandatory counseling sessions, I woke up on the floor, covered in sweat and tears, the prison-assigned therapist patting my face.

When I asked her what happened, she looked at me like I was running a line of bullshit. After realizing I wasn't, she told me I'd flipped out, stood, started pacing in circles, arms wrapped around my chest, begging someone to tell me where I was, how I got here, and why they kept asking me to talk about the killings.

Once, I went totally blank in the kitchen while attempting to prepare dinner. I couldn't remember how to fix spaghetti, why I was doing it, or who all the women in the kitchen were. Total mind-break, like someone took a towel and wiped that section of my brain clean.

At night I'd sit on my bunk, gaze fixed on the spots in the ceiling, and sob. Not just for all I'd lost, but for what I just concluded I was about to lose: My mind. "Just like Mom," I whispered. "Just like Mom."

The conversation with Dr. Critchon played over and over inside my head. "I went ahead and did a full workup on you, including genetic tests, Mrs. Davenport, given your family history. I'm sorry to say the test results indicate you have the genetic markers for autosomal dominant Alzheimer's disease, just like your mother. It's rare and runs in families and tends to show up early in life. You should inform all your blood relatives and have them get tested as well."

Knowing Carol didn't test positive was a blessing, and even though I was still angry at Rebecca, I was glad she didn't have the markers either. Not because of some sudden shift in my opinion of her but because she needed a normal mind to continue to care for Carol and Mom.

The conversation with Carol in the hot tub the night I lied to her and told her the whitewashed version of why her father and I were getting a divorce, roars back.

"There's nothing worse than losing your mind. When I'm old, I want my body to give out, not my brain."

The only sliver of happiness I could find in the situation was that once my thoughts were forever trapped inside the hallways of my mind—just like Mom's were—I wouldn't remember all the pain and sorrow I'd caused the people I loved.

Of course, I couldn't let *that* happen.

One morning I was busy writing in my journal, shocked to discover five months had passed, ignoring the continuous noise around me. My penmanship was atrocious since a new, fun symptom of my disease appeared: Tremors in my hands. It was visiting day, and the entire cell block was abuzz with activity as other inmates tromped down the aisles to the visitation room to see their loved ones.

"Davenport, you've got a visitor."

Looking up from the paper, I grimaced at the guard staring at me from the other side of the bars. I assumed she was joking, since no one had come to see me after the visit with Reginald months ago. "Not funny."

"Not kidding. Get up."

I'd decided weeks ago that it must be a prerequisite to be a hardcore, rude, nasty bitch to apply and be hired as a correction officer. What rock did these women crawl out from under? They had no manners, no social skills, and certainly no traces of femininity. A few even wore men's cologne. I remember someone telling me, once, that the guards in prison were really men trapped inside women's bodies, yet I couldn't recall who told me. Guess it didn't matter who said it. Truth was truth.

"Is it my attorney?"

"Nope. Some hoity-toity society bitch. You know, like you used to be? The kind that looks like she spends all her free time at the salon and drives a Mercedes."

My heart skipped two beats. Could it be? I let the mask of bravado I normally wore slip a little. "Elizabeth Rosenbaum?"

"Yeah, I think that's what her name tag read. Come on, you've got thirty minutes."

Closing the journal, I stood and followed Officer Twatwaffle McBitchy down the aisle to the visitation room. When she opened the door, I gasped.

Sure enough, perched on the edge of a plastic chair sat Liz. She tried her best to hide emotions from her lovely face, but I saw the disgust. Biting my lip, I looked down at my clothes. Faded and wrinkled, the ensemble made me look like a shriveled up pumpkin rotting in an abandoned field.

Orange is not the new black nor is it an appealing color on anything. Period.

The walk across the room seemed to take forever. Liz's gaze flickered back and forth as she took in everything around her, including all the noisy children clamoring for the attention of their incarcerated mothers. She finally spotted me when I was several feet away. Her eyes grew wide with shock.

Stopping in front of the table between us, I tried to give her my best smile. What came out, I'm sure, was a strange smirk. At a loss as to what to say or do, I simply said: "Hey, Liz."

Swallowing several times while blinking back tears, Liz answered: "Hi, Roxy. You, uh, look great."

I'd heard Liz tell some big fibs over the years but that one topped them all. Always the proper wife and citizen—full of grace and wonderful charm—she was doing her best to seem genuine. I burst out laughing. "And you're full of shit. I look like Casper and the Great Pumpkin's bastard offspring."

Tension finally broken; Liz laughed too and stood to hug me. Though brief, it was wonderful. She still smelled the same. Maybe I should ask her if she had some perfume stashed in her purse and to leave it.

"I see your sense of humor is still intact. God, Roxy, I've missed you."

Pointing to the plastic chairs, we both sat and held hands across the table. "I've missed you too, Liz. It's weird—I've wanted to see you yet hoped you'd stay away. I love you but didn't want you to see me like this."

"I'm sorry it took me so long, but all this has been a lot to take in. Plus, I wanted to make sure Carol was okay and all settled in at school."

While studying Liz's face, the memories of taking turns helping each other when our children were little roared back. They made me feel nostalgic and nauseous at the same time. Richard was a senior now, and ever since the kids were in diapers, our plan was to take a Route 66 tour of America once both kids were in college.

"You're the best, you know that? Seriously. Thank you for all you've done for her."

Flicking away a tear, Liz said: "Welcome. She's like my daughter, too, so how could I not?"

"How's she doing?"

"She loves school, but that's not a surprise. The girl's been itching to be a vet ever since the first day you brought the puppy home, remember?"

"Puppy? We never had a dog."

The look on Liz's face was almost funny. It was a weird mixture of confusion and concern. "Ralphie, remember?"

Searching my memories, I tried to picture the Davenport household with a mutt running around. I came up with squat. "Stop teasing me, Liz. Yes, Carol's had her heart set on being a vet, but only because she wanted to be like Rebecca."

Liz furrowed her brow. "You mean Rachel."

A dull headache pressed against my temples and my hands started to shake. "Uh, yeah. Rachel."

Leaning forward, Liz whispered: "What's wrong, Roxy? Are they giving you medication or something because they think you're dangerous?"

A spark of anger made me grit my teeth. I didn't appreciate the stupid game Liz was playing. "Why would you think that, Liz? Is that why you came here? To see how far I've fallen, mock me, say things to confuse me? Did Sasha send you here to spy on me so you could report back to those hags in book club what life is like for me now?"

"Roxy! What a thing to say to me. Of course not. I love you—and I'm not trying to confuse you. In fact, I'm the one who's confused. You had a dog for years named Ralphie. You're the one who mixed up the names of your sisters, not me. I'm sorry, I just assumed the prison had you on some sort of medication that's messing with your memory, that's all."

I started shaking. "God, I'm sorry. I didn't mean to yell. I just—I'm having trouble remembering things—missing sections of time. It freaks me out because I know what it means, and that it won't get any better. Soon, I'll be living in Hell on earth, just like my mom. Remember the day I stepped outside and took that call, right before book club?"

"Yes."

"It wasn't from my lawyer. It was Dr. Critchon, informing me I carry the same genetic marker as Mom."

More tears trickled down Liz's face as she reached out for my hands again. "Oh, Roxy. I'm so sorry. When did you start having symptoms?"

I couldn't look into Liz's beautiful eyes any longer. The pain and regret behind them was too much to handle. Instead, I shifted my gaze out the dirty window—which by the way—needed some Windex asap. "Almost sixteen months ago. Just little episodes here and there, nothing major. That's all changed inside here. It's happening quite frequently now. Not only am I having issues recalling things, but like you just saw, I can't seem to control my anger."

Nodding, Liz replied: "In a weird, sick way, it sort of makes sense now. I mean, I saw the change in you, too, but attributed it to all the stressors in your life. Do you think that's why you—?"

"No," I interrupted, "I'm not blaming my choices on this or on drinking too much. I just snapped that's all. My world exploded in front of my eyes and I lost it. I take full responsibility for the awful things I did."

"I don't agree with what you did, and honestly, part of me hates you for destroying Carol's world. Our friendship. The life we envisioned living as friends and grandparents together. It took a lot for the other part of me who still loves you to win out. That's why I'm here. I needed to tell you I still love you, though I despise your actions, plus let you know I'll always be there for Carol and your mother. Always."

"Guess now's the time for me to tell you how much I love you before I forget who you are," I joked, wiping the tears from my chin.

"Not even funny, Roxy. Not in the least."

We stared at each other, lost inside our pain and communal grief. The mention of my mother made my heart pound. Watching a vibrant woman lose her mind and become nothing more than a body that looked like my mother yet housed a stranger, had been devastating.

There was no way I'd let that happen to those I loved. Period.

"Liz, I appreciate more than I can express you coming to see me. Knowing you'll be there for Carol and my mom means the world to me. Really. You've always been my sister, and what I'm about to say will sound hateful and mean but trust me, it's for your own good. Ha, isn't that trite? My dad used to say that right before spanking us. Too funny."

"Roxy, what are you—?"

Letting go of Liz's hands, I stood. "I'm saying goodbye, Liz. I won't have you watch me wither away to nothing like I did with my mom. It's beyond painful. It's downright gutwrenching. Just think of me as dead, because soon, the Roxy you know will be."

"Roxy! Wait!" Liz yelled.

Turning, I fled the visitation room, tears streaming down my face as I nodded to the guard to let me out. Once in the hallway, the sounds of Liz's voice muffled, I looked at the guard who escorted me to the room earlier. "Make sure to take her name off the approved visitor list."

Sorry, my bestie, but it's for the best.

Trust me.

Today, I have another visitor—four months after the painful interactions with—uh, Liz—yes, that's her name. I was a ball of nerves as I walked into the ghastly visitation room, barely noticing the windows were still in desperate need of a thorough cleaning.

She looked beautiful. Rested. The dark circles under her eyes barely visible, her jet-black hair cut into a short bob tucked back behind dainty ears.

New clothes; new makeup, yet still my beautiful Carol. Today marked nearly nine months since I'd last seen her in the courtroom, transforming my little girl into a grown woman.

When she hugged me, I thought my heart would explode from joy. "Hey, baby. You look wonderful. I love the new haircut. How's school?"

"Fine. Grades could be better, but fine."

"Give yourself a break, sweetie. You've got a lot of things to concentrate on, not just school."

"True, and I am."

Awkward silence settled over us. Carol's green eyes clouded over with tears as she took in my disheveled appearance. Though I had no scale, I knew I'd lost weight since my clothes hung on me like rags.

"I miss you, Mom, and I deserve to be right—"

"No, you don't. You're right where you're supposed to be. College, a job, and moving on with life."

"I'm so sorry for what I did. I was just so angry that night after Dad told me about Ginger and the baby. I couldn't think straight after reading your journal, and like a fool I left it—"

"Shhh, baby. It's time to walk away from past mistakes and move forward."

A few tears leaked from the corners of her eyes, slowly gliding down rosy cheeks. "I'm trying, but it's really hard, Mom. Really hard. What we did was wrong."

Reaching out across the plastic table, I took Carol's hand in mine. They were warm, soft, with a faint hint of lemongrass, courtesy of her favorite hand lotion. "I know, but you're strong. You can and will make it. You're still going to counseling, right?"

Carol nodded. "Yes. Dr. Smithers is great. He's helping me cope and so is Mr. Greenwood, Aunt Becca and Liz."

"Good! You haven't told Dr. Smithers or Liz everything, right? Only discuss the real issues with Reginald and Rachel?"

Worry lines creased her brow. "You mean Aunt Rebecca."

"What?"

"You said Rachel."

"I did? Oh, sorry. Yes, I meant Rebecca. Answer my question, please. You haven't told anyone who shouldn't know, right?"

"Of course I haven't. Dr. Smithers and Liz would freak, and Mr. Greenwood is a great listener. He even helped me with my first report in English. Nice guy, for a lawyer."

"Yes, he is," I commented, unwilling to mention Reginald wasn't being nice out of the kindness of his heart.

"Aunt Becca and Liz have been wonderful, Mom. Aunt Becca's even teaching me accounting so I can handle my finances. She sold Grandma's house last month and put the money in a trust fund for me. Oh, and she bought me a new laptop last week so I can work from the dorm."

A random memory of my youth appeared, of me taking Rebecca's dolls outside in the dead of night, cutting all their hair off then tearing their little plastic limbs off and burying them in the backyard. How I'd giggled under the moonlight as I destroyed things I knew Rebecca loved—and how, when Daddy caught me one night, he took the shovel and dug the hole deeper, all while talking calmly to me about what I was doing was wrong. In a stern yet gentle voice, he said he understood I didn't love Rebecca, that sibling rivalry was a normal, natural feeling, but I would have to suck it up and keep a smile on my face, hiding my real feelings from others. "That's what we do, Roxy. People like you and me—full of thoughts we shouldn't have—we tuck them away deep inside, keeping them from others. It's best that way."

I took his words to heart and followed the rule ever since that night. Great advice, Dad. All the bottled emotions escaped at one time, leaving a trail of misery and heartache in its wake.

God, I'd been a sick, twisted person my entire life yet hid the dark side for years. I hope the new owners don't decide to put in a pool. They would be in for a shock at what little hidden treasures are buried in the yard—the ones I didn't have time to remove.

Thinking about burying things made me shudder. It had been almost a year and no detectives had come around, questioning me about the whereabouts of Benny Rogers. Was it possible I'd actually gotten away with that one? Wouldn't it be the sickest twist ever if I had, and then once my mind completely faded, I spilled the beans?

That was a risk I wasn't willing to take. Carol had no idea this would be her first—and final—visit. Reaching inside my pocket, I felt a wave of calm settle over me when I touched the small package of salted peanuts I'd snagged from the kitchen.

"Mom? Are you okay?"

"Uh, yes. Just thinking about all the years I spent in that house and how I'm sort of glad I won't be able to see someone else living in it. So, you said you aren't working at the vet's office anymore?"

"No. Dr. Varner couldn't handle all the media attention. Frankly, neither could I, so I quit right after you went to court."

"I'm sorry, honey. I know how much you loved working with the animals. But soon, you'll be your own boss and have your own clinic. Nobody will take that away from you. That's a promise."

"It's okay, Mom. Really."

"So, what kind of work are you doing from the dorm?"

"Data entry in QuickBooks for some of Aunt Becca's clients. Easy stuff."

"That's good, sweetie. Just don't overextend yourself. School comes first."

"I know, Mom," Carol answered, frowning. "I've learned a lot of techniques about how to handle stress from Dr. Smithers. Plus, the advice he shares with me works, no matter the underlying reasons of insanity, or his lack of knowledge about what I did."

"Honey, you aren't insane. What happened isn't your fault—it's mine. I'm so sorry I wasn't a better role model."

"Bullshit, Mom. You were—and still are—a great role model. Look what you sacrificed for me—"

"Shhh, Carol. Certain things don't need to be discussed. Not here. You never know if ears are listening."

"I don't care, Mom! What you did for me—and how I just kept my mouth shut and didn't stand up and take responsibility for my own actions—it haunts me. Every single day. It was the ultimate act of love on your part, and the epitome of cowardice on mine. Look how long it took me to come see you? I mean, what kind of daughter am I?"

The sweet voice, full of lovely, heartfelt words, continued to buzz around me, but they didn't make sense. My head hurt, and my heart pounded in my chest. I tried, but couldn't, take a deep breath, like someone had their arms clamped around my chest.

Where am I?

Why am I dressed in these orange, ugly, itchy clothes?

God, it stinks in here. Did I forget to take out the garbage?

Why is this young woman across from me crying? She's talking nonsense and keeps calling me mom.

The walls of the room closed in. In a state of panic, I jerked my hand from the strange girl's and stood. "Stop calling me that! I don't know you. Where am I? Who are you? What's going on? Why does it smell so awful in here?"

"Mom? Oh, my God! Mom! What's wrong?"

"Get away from me!" I screamed, pushing the strange girl away.

"Help! Someone, we need a doctor. I think Mom's having a heart attack or stroke! Hurry!"

Knocking the table over in an attempt to scramble away from the crazy strangers, I ran to the corner of the unfamiliar room. Crumpling into a heap, sobbing uncontrollably, I felt the arms of the young woman embrace me.

"Shhh, Mom. It's okay. I'm here. Just breathe. Deep, slow breaths. That's it."

Something about her voice was soothing. The calming scent

of lemongrass seemed familiar. Whatever it was, the panic inside my mind eased up enough for me to let the kind girl hold me, while softly humming in my ear.

She was very nice, even though she was confused. Poor girl thinks I'm her mother and isn't that just the saddest thing?

Opening my eyes, I looked down at the dirty floor.

Yikes, it was a mess.

The housewife responsible for this untidy, ugly home deserved a demerit.

***

"Well, it's about time you woke up. Girl, lots of inmates are pissed off at you for ruining visiting day. I would suggest you stay in your cell for a few days before venturing out into gen pop."

Looking at the staff nurse who looked about as happy to be in the prison infirmary as I was, I smirked. "I'm feeling fine, thank you. Not that you care, obviously, just thought I'd throw it out there. Where's my daughter? Is she still here?"

"Like everyone else, when visiting hours are over, they're over. No special privileges for anyone—period."

If my left hand wasn't shackled to the bed … "How long have I been out?"

Staring at me with dead eyes (again, what rocks does the state turn over to find these women?) Nurse Crabapple looked at me as though I was an annoying bug on her sleeve. "Long enough for shift change. I just got here and need to make my rounds. When I return, I'll take you back to your cell."

Forcing my face to remain neutral, I nodded, damn near giddy when I noticed the package of peanuts was on the tray, just close enough for me to reach.

With exceptional patience, I waited until I couldn't hear the *squish-squash* of her shoes down the hallway. Leaning over, I snatched the package of peanuts, tore off the edge then chomped and swallowed, relishing the taste I hadn't experienced since I was four.

My goodness, I'd forgotten how amazing peanuts tasted. Too bad they were highly toxic to my system.

Within seconds, I felt my chest tighten and pulse race. Heat raced through my body, followed by horrible stomach cramps. I fought through all the anaphylactic reactions, unwilling to alert Nurse Crabapple so she could swoop in and save me.

No, not this time. It's time for Raging Roxy to take her secrets to the grave and to rest.

Permanently.

Goodbyes had already been said to Carol and Liz, and I refused to risk the sacrifice I made for my daughter, in case my mind slipped and betrayed her—or accidently incriminated myself about Benny-Boo one day. I had no intention of her watching my mind slowly disintegrate into that of a stranger's, because I knew from personal experience how truly heartbreaking that was to witness.

No way. That would be the ultimate demerit, and I've got enough in my jar for eternity.

As my eyes started to swell, I had one last clear thought. Glancing back over to the tray, I spotted a black marker. Grabbing it, my fingers trembling, I scrawled *Suburbia Made Me Do It* across my left forearm, a devious smile across my lips as I looked at my horrid penmanship.

I tried to whisper, "I love you, Carol Claire," but my swollen tongue wouldn't allow it. Grabbing the handrail, I closed my eyes and didn't fight the convulsions as I carried out my self-imposed death penalty.

Roxy's Final Rule: Do whatever it takes to protect Carol.

Nailed it!

EPILOGUE

Tainted Fruit

"It's almost time for their services, Carol. Are you finished with your notes for the eulogy? Also, did you want to go first, or do you want me to start with Grandma's? It's your choice, honey."

Sighing, Carol forced her voice to remain calm as her new nemesis stepped into the family preparation room. "I don't need notes to say what's on my mind, Aunt Becca. I'll wing it; be blunt, to the point and honest—just like Mom would do. Feel free to go first with Grandma's eulogy."

"Sure thing. I'm as ready as I'll ever be," Rebecca responded, casually glancing at the nearly empty room across the hallway where the services would soon start. "Are you sure you really want to put yourself through the emotional wringer, sweetie? There are less than ten people sitting in the parlor. Maybe we should just forgo the formalities, you take the urns home rather than to the cemetery, and we can then put this whole nightmare behind us for good?"

"No way." Carol fought back the rage consuming her mind. During the two days after learning of her mother's suicide and her grandmother's sudden heart attack within twenty minutes of each other, Carol's thoughts were full of dark, ugly scenarios, just as they'd been the night she'd killed her piece-of-shit father and his whore after Daddy-Dearest dropped the horrible news during dinner about the *real* reason behind the end of the marriage.

What little relationship she had with her father ended when he had the nerve to introduce Ginger as his *future* wife then broke the news about their baby. He'd tried to make it sound like an exciting adventure, one he wanted her to be a part of as the "big sis."

Grief and disgust drove her to the edge of insanity, which she then took out on the May–December couple with the aid of an 8" butcher knife—a plot planted inside her mind the minute she fled home and found her mother passed out on the bathroom floor—a small notebook clasped between bloodstained fingers, a plastic sack full of bloody clothes, and an empty pill bottle resting near the commode.

She'd slumped to the floor and started reading, the words sometimes difficult to decipher each time her eyes welled up with tears. Fury at her father, along with a smidge of anger at her mother for lying to her, attempting to shield her from the news, dried the tears away.

No: Rage burned them away.

For months after her mother's incarceration, Carol tried to work through her feelings with the therapist, Aunt Rebecca, and a few times with Reginald Greenwood. Like a naïve fool, she assumed the interactions helped.

They did—for a while.

All the progress vanished when her mother's secret journal landed in her hands, pushing her right over the precipice, sending Carol straight into the bowels of her twisted, demented mind.

When a representative from the prison called, informing Carol of her mother's passing, she'd raced back to the prison, her broken heart already in tatters after witnessing her mother's earlier break with reality. She'd been stuck inside a small waiting room for hours, filled out stacks of paperwork and then met with a grief counselor, who handed her a small sack filled with her mother's personal belongings.

Driving home late that night, she'd sobbed the entire way, mentally shredding her pathetic self apart for waiting so long to visit, and for her own actions spurring her mother's.

Yet once she arrived home and pilfered through the bag, Carol's life trajectory took a sharp nosedive when she found the tattered, dirty notebook.

She'd read every single word scribbled on the fragile pieces of paper written in shaky cursive. Her mother's once-lovely handwriting deteriorated almost as fast as her mind, turning what was once something beautiful into a jumbled, almost unrecognizable mess.

Reading all the new knowledge about the truth of her entire family and the fact her mother killed Benny and later, herself, to keep Carol safe, turned her heart into a solid piece of stone. Her mother had always been an obsessive note taker, yet knowing her mind slipped so fast she didn't even remember keeping the words, falsely recalling she'd write then toss into the toilet, made Carol shake her head at the senseless of it all.

And, it formed a new plan—a new life goal and purpose—within hours after reading the last entry. The first item on the agenda: take a few of her mother's favorite dresses and the journal full of the ugly, disgusting truth to the funeral home and have them burned right along with her mother, forever destroying the truth in a ball of flames.

***

Pulling her maniacal thoughts back to the present, Carol nodded toward the door, ignoring the look of annoyance on Aunt Becca's face.

No, not Aunt Becca. Lunatic Bitch.

With a fake smile, Carol fell in to step behind L.B. "I wish you could join me after the services at Eternal Slumber Acres. It's going to be weird burying their urns alone."

Rebecca stopped, brow furrowing with irritation. "I'm sorry, Carol, but I told you I simply cannot change this meeting. I've been fighting for months about this and I've got to get things settled or we'll end up in mediation—or worse. I've already got enough on my plate to deal with and then those idiots try and back out of the deal. I'm beyond ready to finalize things and have the issue of Grandma's house off my plate."

Carol stiffened, unable to hide the look of anger from her face.

"Honey, don't look at me like that. I'm sorry, really. None of this has been easy on me, either. Why don't you wait until tomorrow to take the urns? I'll be able to go with you and we can bury them in private, okay? Maybe go shopping afterwards? Retail therapy does wonders for the soul."

"Okay," Carol responded in a quiet whisper. "Just the two of us—our little secret. Right?"

Planting a light kiss on Carol's soft cheek, Rebecca said: "Just between us girls, I promise."

The sounds of faint organ music filled the small room as they entered. Carol spotted Liz and her family near the front. She let Rebecca go first to the podium then slid into the stiff pew next to Liz.

"Hey, baby girl. You doing okay?" Liz asked, slipping an arm over Carol's shoulder.

Nodding, Carol didn't say a word as she half-heartedly listened to Lunatic Bitch jabber on about her feelings about her deceased mother and sister.

She didn't have the inclination to listen—she was too busy planning out how things would go down at Eternal Slumber Acres the next day when it was just aunt and niece.

Alone.

Two would arrive; only one would leave. The other would remain, joining Benny's corpse forever.

Biting her cheek to keep from smiling, Carol knew there was no doubt: she was her mother's daughter.

ACKNOWLEDGEMENTS

There are so many people I need to thank yet it would take an entire novel to list them all. However, there are some very special people I wish to thank:

To my family: You all have been my rocks during the last six years! Mom, you even decided to join the madness and penned two novels with me! My dear husband, you've endured all the craziness, my bouts of anxiety, late nights typing away at the computer as each story poured out of me. Thank you, Michael, for being such an amazing man. Mom and Frankie--the two of you have been my biggest cheerleaders, encouraging me to continue on when I felt like giving up. And son, you are, and always have been, my reason for living. Your strength and determination inspires me each and every day. Dad and Cindy: your love and continued support as I navigated my way through the numerous perils of this journey is appreciated more than I can say. Allison, Brittney and Lindsey: the three of you bring tremendous joy to my life and I love you all as though you were my own. My heart belongs to each and every one of you.

Jeff LaFerney: Author and friend. You have the patience of a saint, a heart of gold, and a brilliant way with words. When life's woes buried me under a pile of mental rubble, your hand was the first to poke through the debris. You are a man of faith, family and morals—a rare combination in the world today. It is an honor to call you friend.

Sabrina Stewart: You are more than an actress, voice-over artist, producer and director. You are a beautiful soul with enough passion and drive to sustain a roomful of people for their lifetimes! Love and warmth radiate from you like a beacon in the darkness. You share a special place in my heart because you believed enough in my writing to take on the monumental task of creating not one but two films based on my books. Your love for mankind and desire to create memorable works inspire me every single day.

Andrea Emmes: Your talent is boundless! Your angelic voice gave the breath of life to words on a page above and beyond my wildest expectations. So much emotion and passion oozes out of you like sweet, raw honey. Every single time I listened to a chapter loaded up to ACX a lump of tears formed in my throat, completely awed by your talents to *be* the characters from my imagination. Your strong faith and kind demeanor speak volumes of about your love for God.

Sara Morsey: Strong, confident and artistic, you are a woman who knows how to take charge and live each day to the fullest. You've been with me on this journey from the very beginning, encouraging me to keep writing, keep digging deep for inspiration and to keep pounding the words out. Your vocal range astounds me with each book you've narrated for me. No one can pull off the sexy southern dialect like you do!

Rebecca Roberts: Tough and full of spunk, you are honest about your thoughts and opinions, urging me to step out of my comfort zone and believe in my work as much as you did. Without your backbone of support and insistence I seek out an agent to take things to the next level, I wouldn't have had the guts to write *Marriage Made Me Do It.* The one little sentence you spoke in a phone conversation changed my life: "Your sense of humor is wickedly funny so you should write a dark comedy." I took the challenge and look what happened! You kicked me out of my comfortable nest, forcing me to fly. Now, we are soaring together.

Elaine Raco Chase: Mentor and personal confidant—you are a cheerleader extraordinaire! With a smile and a loving spirit, you have been a staunch supporter from day one and a loyal friend. Witty, charming, and with a wicked sense of humor, we clicked from the beginning and haven't slowed down since. My ears are always ready to listen to your sage advice and playful banter.

Janelle Taylor: Inspiration is the first word that comes to mind when I think about you, followed by the close second of determination. You have the heart of a true steel magnolia. The love you have for the craft of writing and the heights you've achieved during your glorious career are inspirational. One of the first people I ever interviewed on my radio show, I recall how nervous I was to speak with you—until your sweet, Georgia-tinged voice assured me things would be just fine—and they were after you graciously walked *me* through interviewing *you.* Just like Elaine Raco Chase, you've been an avid supporter, encouraging me to continue on, and that means the world to me.

Linda Langton: Superwoman. That is my nickname for you, Linda. You went above and beyond the duties of a literary agent. You took time to assist me from start to finish in a world I was unfamiliar with, encouraging me throughout the entire process, helping me achieve a dream I've had for years. Thank you for everything. Your cape is in the mail. J

Betty Dravis: Like Elaine and Janelle, you've been a part of this crazy journey with me since the minute I took my first step on the path of writing. Like an archaeologist, you looked past the dirt and debris of the unpolished words, recognizing the hidden treasure just below the surface. With gentle urging and reassurances the raw talent just needed some spot cleaning, you've been my rock. Thank you for the guidance, friendship, and most importantly for being you. When God fashioned you, He broke the mold.

Joanna Lee Doster: My New York Soul Sister! Your friendship and encouragement mean more to me than I can properly put into words. We've shared so many wonderful moments over the years and countless hours on the phone while swapping stories, tips, ideas and more. Allow me to publicly apologize for giving you nightmares as I read chapters from my zombie series to you over the phone, and thank you for being such a wonderful soundboard as I hash out new plots and tales. For you, the world.

Donna Lickteig, Donna Thompson, and Pam Carroway Jones: Better known as "Ashley's Angels" because of the role all three of you have played in my life. Support, encouragement and friendship to boot—books drew us together yet our comradery will keep us connected. Allow me to express my heartfelt thanks to all three of you for being a part of my life and walking alongside me on this journey.

Kathryn Cheshire, Editor, Killer Reads: Words cannot aptly express how thankful I am for your expert guidance, superior patience and belief in my work. You are a treasure and I hope one day to meet you face-to-face and give you a hug!

To my fans: You didn't think I'd forgotten about all of you, right? Of course I didn't! Each and every one of you and all the downloads, reviews, shares, tweets, comments and support made all the falls and stumbles during the past six years tolerable and the reason I kept going!

Tomorrow is promised to none—embrace the present and say what's on your heart to those who've made your time here on this planet memorable. Pass along the gratitude to the lives of others and guess what? You'll discover a whole new attitude in your own.

KILLER READS

DISCOVER THE BEST IN CRIME AND THRILLER

Follow us on social media to get to know the team behind the books, enter exclusive giveaways, learn about the latest competitions, hear from our authors, and lots more:

CPSIA information can be obtained
at www.ICGtesting.com
Printed in the USA
LVHW03s2005160718
583907LV00010B/464/P